# THE KEEPING PLACE

## BETTY JACKSON CUTLER

PublishAmerica
Baltimore

First printing

At the specific preference of the author, PublishAmerica allowed this work to remain exactly as the author intended, verbatim, without editorial input.

ISBN: 1-4241-0139-5
PUBLISHED BY PUBLISHAMERICA, LLLP
www.publishamerica.com
Baltimore

Printed in the United States of America

## DEDICATION

This book is a work of fiction, but my inspiration for writing this book came nearly twenty years ago from the true story of a young girl who went into a coma from an accidental drug overdose. There was a court battle waged to take her off life support. Her parents won the court decision. She was placed in a care center to live out the rest of her life. I lost track of her shortly after that. Your young life was lost, and for this reason, I dedicate this to you, Kathleen Quinlin, wherever you are.

To Mel,
a good friend + fan,

Betty J Cutler
2006

## ACKNOWLEDGEMENTS

I would like to thank my daughter, Karla Rouska, for sacrificing the many hours it took to help me edit, re-edit, and edit again so I could get this book published, and for the laughter we shared during the process.

I would also like to thank my good friends, Larry Nielson, Nedra Thompson, Bertha Anderson, Corey Gonzales, Sharon Fisher, Marty Luther, and Sue Stone who read and constructively critiqued my manuscript, and gave me the encouragement I needed.

# CHAPTER ONE

Laurel stumbled, unable to catch herself, she fell to the ground landing hard on both her hands and knees. She shook her head, turned around and sat on the pavement. For a moment, she couldn't focus, and then, as she regained her balance she saw that she was sitting in the middle of a deserted highway. Dazed and disoriented, she slowly rose to a standing position. Feeling very self-conscious, she looked down at her sore and bruised body expecting to find cuts and scratches, but there were none. Her pants were ripped at the knee from the fall, but to all outward appearances, she seemed to be all right. She ached all over, and felt like she was about to cry.

"Where am I?" she said aloud, as she looked around to see if she recognized anything. Everything looked strange. Trees, like silhouettes, lined both sides of the highway. She thought how strange everything was, not quite comprehending what she was seeing and feeling. Afraid of hearing her own voice echo in this strange place again, she kept silent, but unfamiliar thoughts raced through her head, thoughts that seemed to have no reality.

She started walking aimlessly, staggering a little, as she walked. In the distance, she thought she could see a building, or something. It was hard to see exactly what it was through the mist that had mysteriously appeared. Whatever it was it looked small, but that, she thought, *could be an illusion of the distance.* While she walked, she kept her eyes transfixed on this strange object, hoping she could figure out what it was. Being completely disoriented, it gave her some direction to head toward. There wasn't anything around it. No other buildings were there, no trees or shrubs. It stood alone. Nothing was around it but empty space. It was almost colorless, with black frames around the windows and a door. There was a sign above the front door on the roof, but she was still too far away to make out the letters. Her curiosity was growing, but not more than her fear.

In this transfixed state of mind, she walked toward the strange apparition feeling like she was on a treadmill, but she kept moving at a steady pace. She had no idea where she was, or why she was here, but she was sure, there was something terribly wrong. As she walked, she tried to remember what she had been doing before she found herself in this situation. Then in an instant, the memory flashed through her mind.

She had been driving down the freeway in her new car on her way to meet her business partner, Kim. Having just purchased the first new car she had ever owned, a pearlized mauve-colored sports car convertible, she was anxious to show it off to Kim. She was driving, maybe a little too fast, the top was down, with the wind blowing through her raven hair, she felt sensuous as she closed her eyes just for a second to enjoy the freedom of that wonderful moment. Now, she thought frantically, *what had happened?* Here she was lost in this place, on this highway to nowhere, and there was no one, anywhere, to help her. She was totally alone.

She began to face the frightening reality that she was not in control of her own destiny. A force that she could not describe appeared to be controlling her movements. She ambled on thinking strange thoughts. At least her thoughts seemed to be her own, even though, they seemed distracted and fragmented. It was hard to keep her mind on anything particular. She wondered why she was walking on the side of the road because, the long thin heels of her shoes kept sticking in the soft tar along the shoulder. She might as well be walking down the middle of this strange highway since there hadn't been a car along in all the while she had been walking. She decided to take off her shoes and carry them by the heel straps as she trudged along. Feeling more weary than she had ever felt in her life, she walked on with a purpose, unknown even to herself.

Laurel seemed to understand that reaching the building that had appeared in the mist was her only hope of finding someone, anyone, who might be able to help her. The tears she had been trying to hold back started streaming down her face. She reached down to pull up the tail of her blouse, and with it wiped away the tears, smudging black mascara on it and on her face. She reasoned that crying wasn't going to help. She didn't know what to feel anymore. She only knew there was a blanket of fear lingering around her, ready at any moment to wrap itself around her body and smother her. She couldn't let that happen. She stopped walking, regained her composure, and with more determination than ever started to run toward the distant building.

Laurel made up her mind that nothing was going to keep her from reaching that building even if she had to crawl. Running, then walking, and then running again whenever she could find the strength for what seemed like hours. A strange dizziness would sometimes overtake her, and she would have to stop and rest. As she got closer, she could see the building more clearly. It looked like a place of business. Maybe, it was a store or a cafe. When she finally reached it, and was standing just outside the building, she stood there for a few minutes staring, almost in suspended animation, wondering what she should do, hoping she would find an answer to this bizarre situation that she had been thrust into. Then, as if being pushed from behind, she approached the door. She reached for the handle, when the door opened, by itself. Standing in the doorway was a pleasant looking woman who appeared to be in her early forties.

"Come right on in, young lady," she said, reaching out to Laurel with both hands, "You look like you've had a rough time." Laurel hadn't thought of what she must look like. She looked down at her rumpled blouse, as she reached out to grasp this person's outstretched hands. When she left her house this morning she had been perfectly groomed, wearing a cream-colored silk blouse with long sleeves and black pants. Her shoes were black sling back heels that she now carried in one hand. As she looked down, she could see that her once spotless blouse was wrinkled and smudged with a combination of mascara and dirt. From walking on the pavement without her shoes, holes had worn through the thin nylon stockings she was wearing, and her toes were protruding through the fabric until she was almost barefooted.

"I guess I must look a mess," she said absently. She felt her cheeks flush. Tears welled up in her eyes, and the fear that had been lingering inside her suddenly engulfed her as she slumped to the floor, still holding onto the woman's hands. Before she knew what was happening, she began to tremble uncontrollably. The room with its sudden quietness became a terrifying nightmare that threatened to squeeze the very life out of her. Deep, gasping sobs quickly took control of her body as she slipped into complete darkness.

When Laurel regained consciousness, she heard strange sounds. The noises sounded like dishes clanking together. She lay perfectly still, and her eyes opened slowly. She was in a dark room. The shades had been pulled down to keep out the light. She sat up on an old gray couch, which she had been placed upon. Her head was throbbing. For a long time she sat there leaning forward, covering her face with her hands. The memory of what had happened in the cafe came rushing back to her. She stood up carefully, looked around the dark shabby room, and slowly headed for the sounds she could hear in the next room. She decided that she must be in the back room of the cafe. There was a colorful floral curtain hung where the door should have been, separating her from what she assumed must be the kitchen. She was about to lift the curtain when the woman she had seen earlier came in, pushing it aside.

Startled, Laurel backed away as the woman said, "Are you feelin' better now, Honey? My name is Nora Sanders, and my husband, Ed, and I are the proprietors of this cafe. We'd like to help you if we can. Sit down and I'll get you some nice hot tea, and somethin' to eat. Are you hungry?"

Laurel started to speak, but then sat back down on the couch and nodded yes to the question. Actually, she was famished, but until this very moment, she hadn't had time to think about being hungry. These strange sensations inside her head and body were very frightening, and she had such a feeling of being completely alone. Even though this woman seemed nice enough, she was still a complete stranger, and Laurel had no idea what was going on. Usually, she was in complete control of her emotions, but something was very wrong here. For the time being, she wasn't quite sure how to handle what was happening to her.

Nora gave Laurel something to eat, a small crustless ham and cheese sandwich and a glass of milk, and then left her alone again in the back room. Laurel kept thinking, *What am I going to do? Where am I? And, who are these people?* She could feel herself about to panic again. Tears filled her eyes, and she felt as if she were choking as her throat swelled with fear. *I can't do this! I can't behave this way,* she thought. *I have to think rationally.* She took a deep breath and tried to calm herself. Gradually her throat returned to normal, and the tears subsided enough for her to begin to gather her thoughts.

"I must find out where I am." she said aloud. As if somehow, saying it aloud would help her make more sense of what had happened? With renewed composure, she brushed her hair back, and started for the kitchen. *There must be a phone, I'll call Kim,* she thought. *She must be worried sick about me by now. I was supposed to meet her at 2 o'clock! It must be a least five or 6 o'clock.*

Laurel walked through the kitchen, and headed for the half double doors that appeared to lead to the dining room. She stood in the open doorway for a moment surveying the room. People sat at tables and booths, completely oblivious to her, laughing and talking. She tried to make some sense of this place, this situation, but nothing she could think of seemed to justify any of this. Across the room, a black wall phone hung on a brown paneled wall. As she crossed the room toward the phone, Nora called out to her. "Laurel honey, I'm glad to see you're feelin' a little better." Laurel glanced over her shoulder, but kept walking toward the phone.

"Ya, yeah," she stuttered, "I'm feeling better, thanks. I just thought I would call a friend, to let her know I'm all right." She fumbled through her pockets to get a quarter for the phone. Suddenly, digging deeper she realized she didn't have any money at all, no identification, nothing! She thought, *I've lost my purse! I'm sure it was in the car when I left home.* Laurel knew she had brought it from home. She distinctly remembered laying it on the front seat when she got into the car this afternoon. She suddenly realized that she didn't know where her car was.

"My car! My beautiful new car! Where's my car?" she asked

almost screaming. Until now, she hadn't given a thought to where her car might be. She had no idea where she left it. She walked over to Nora. "I must be losing my mind!" she said. "I had a car! Where is my car? All of my identification, my purse, my car, everything is gone!" Obvious panic was beginning to move in on her. Her voice was becoming high pitched and strained. Nora grabbed Laurel by the shoulders and shook her slightly.

"Now, listen here, you've got to get hold of yourself, and right now!" Nora had to hold back her emotions, trying to control the situation. She didn't want to slap the girl, but she felt that Laurel was close to hysterics and that would only make matters worse.

"We'll find your car, I promise. We'll start looking for your car as soon as we close the cafe. And, in the meantime, why don't you freshen up. You can use the room in the back. There's a shower and everything you'll need." Nora put her arm around Laurel, and started to lead her to the back room.

"I...I...I need to make a phone call," Laurel pleaded, trying to pull away. For a moment, she had the feeling she was being held against her will, and wondered why they would not want her to leave. *They seem to be trying to keep me here,* she thought. She realized that she was confused, but going home or contacting someone she knew would obviously relieve those feelings, and they should be aware of this too. They apparently did not want to let her go. *But, of course, that was nonsense,* she thought, and she was too tired and upset to argue with Nora anymore. She was led to the back room, again, as Nora tried to reassure her that everything was all right.

"Alright, Alright," Nora said as calmly as she could, trying not to frighten Laurel. "You go freshen up first, and then you can call your friends." Laurel did not want to wait, but thought maybe, she would feel more comfortable and more rational if she were cleaned up. For some reason, she felt dirty, and now the thought of cleaning herself made her think that maybe she really could wash away this whole mess, wipe it away clean, and it would all go away down the drain like some bad dream, or nightmare to be more specific. In her mind she kept saying, *when will I wake up?* And then, she had a fleeting thought. *I didn't tell this woman...this "Nora," my name. How did she know my name?* Laurel thought. *I don't know this woman...I've never seen her in my life, but somehow, this woman knows me!*

# CHAPTER TWO

Kim, Laurel's friend and business partner, had been waiting for half an hour at the River Boat Cafe. This was where she and Laurel had planned to meet on this particular afternoon. It was one of the best eating establishments around town, and they ate there often. The food there was fantastic, and the Crab Louie was "to die" for. But now, Kim was getting worried. She began wondering if she had the time right. *Could there have been a misunderstanding? Surely, Laurel would have called me if she were going to be late,* Kim thought. She was surprised at the foreboding she felt. It seemed more than the usual feelings of anxiety she would feel when someone was late, or missed an appointment. She tried to dismiss the feeling thinking, *it must be my imagination.* She was becoming very concerned, even though she thought she was being silly and overly worrisome. It was a trait of hers to worry more than she needed to over relatively little things. However, maybe that was what made her push so hard to do things right.

Kim was from a very well to do family. She always had all the money she needed. Her grandfather, Karl Donalson, struck it rich in the Gold, Silver and Uranium mines in the West, mostly in California and Utah. After most of the mines had petered out, or had become too dangerous to mine any longer, he moved his family to St. Louis where they had lived ever since in the proverbial "House on the Hill."

Karl, a striking man with blond hair and a muscular build, was sure that if he and his partners had found more investors willing to take the risk, there was definitely more money to be made in the mines. The Uranium mines were particularly dangerous to work in, and he was lucky that he still had his health. He had worked hard and invested well. His wife had made him promise that when he struck it rich they would move to the city, and he had stuck to that promise.

He had made more money than he could spend in a lifetime while he was involved with the mining industry, and he was ready, along

14

with his wife and children, to live a more sophisticated lifestyle. He wanted his children to know what high society was all about. It was time to leave the West and move further east, but he only got as far as the Midwest. An opportunity arose in St. Louis. He packed up his family, took his money, and started a new business venture there.

Karl went into the retail trade business, opening a small store that carried everything anyone would want from hardware to groceries, and even some clothing. It was a variety store that he expanded several times to meet the needs of the people. He had done well. The Donalson name held the respect of everyone who dealt with him. His son, Karl Jr., and granddaughter, Kim, had continued the legacy. Even though they were wealthy, Karl Jr., who had taken after his father in stature and integrity, had never indulged his daughter's whims. He made her learn the trade just as his father had done before with him. He taught her she could do anything she wanted to with hard work, honesty and integrity. She was a good student.

Kim spent many hours in the store as a little girl watching how things were sold and bartered. When Kim's grandfather retired, Kim's dad, Karl Jr., took over the business. Kim worked for her dad from the time she was 12. She started in the stock room sweeping floors, and cleaning bathrooms. As she proved her worth, she was allowed to advance to the sales floor as a clerk. She even spent time working on paperwork, and ordering merchandise. She frequently went on buying trips across the country with her father.

When Kim decided to break out on her own, she could have had her father finance her, but she was too independent for that. In order to do this, though, she would need a partner. And, preferably one that could put up some of the money for the investment. And, that was Laurel.

Kim met Laurel one day while they were each jogging in the park. Kim exercised there often, and sometimes just sat on the grass enjoying life. It was a good release from the pressures of a workday. On this particularly warm summer day, she wore her favorite red jogging shorts and a loose fitting T-shirt. She was a good jogger and usually passed everyone on the path, and in her own way felt quite smug about that, until the day she encountered Laurel. Just as Kim was about to pass her on the jogging path, Laurel went into second gear, and the race was on. Neither would let the other pass. When they finally stopped, neck and neck, and winded almost to exhaustion, Kim held out her hand and introduced herself.

Panting, she said, "Hi, I'm Kim Donalson, and you are?"

After wiping the sweat from her hand onto her blue jogging pants, Laurel reached for Kim's hand, hardly able to catch her breath, smiled and said, "Laurel, Laurel Richards.

They both had their hands on their waists, half-leaning over, and breathing heavily. In a city where it's often hard to meet your next-door neighbor, this was quite a surprise for both of them, even though St. Louis being in the Midwest was friendlier than most cities. Laurel, having just moved to the St. Louis area from Chicago, had always been health conscious. She thought she would probably join a gym, but had not made that commitment yet. Running in the park had been her only form of exercise for the past few weeks, and she was anxious to find someone with her same interests. The park was just a few blocks from her apartment, and she had been enjoying this change of pace. Meeting Kim this way was, perhaps, a positive turn for her new life in St. Louis.

They stopped running next to a park bench, and both nearly fell on it in exhaustion, leaning back still breathing in long labored breaths. As their breathing returned to normal, they looked at each other, and then spontaneously started laughing. Laurel's black shoulder length hair was pulled back with a clip, and Kim had her long blond hair in loose braids. They looked like a couple of high-school cheerleaders working out before school, and the levity of the moment gave way to the kind of laughter that takes your breath away. This kind of connection with a complete stranger was priceless for both of them.

"Can you believe what we just did?" Kim said, when she was finally able to control her laughter.

"No, that was pretty ridiculous, wasn't it?" Laurel said, still laughing too.

They continued talking and found they lived fairly close to each other. Of course, that would account for both of them being in this same park

"I run here about three days a week, whenever I have the time," Kim said. "Maybe we should run on the same days together. It sure would be a lot more interesting. I don't know about you, but since I'm not particularly in tune with nature, I find running to be a little boring at times. I do this for my health, and not necessarily to bond with Mother Nature, although, we're pretty close." Laurel laughed enjoying Kim's sense of humor as she continued, "I realize we don't really know each other, but hey! How do friendships start anyway? By-the-way, have you lived here in St. Louis long?" Kim asked.

"No, actually I just moved here from Chicago. You're the first person I've met since I got here, other than the people I work with, and I *would* prefer running with someone. In fact, I would feel safer. How about you, have you lived here long?"

"Well, yeah. My whole life, right here in good ol' St. Louis," Kim added. "My grandfather settled us here years ago. And, it's been a good life. I have no complaints."

Laurel had a busy schedule, and needed to get to work. She said, "Why don't we meet here again tomorrow morning…about the same time, Okay?"

"Sure, I'll see you tomorrow," Kim said, as she headed off to her apartment and prepared to go to work at her father's store. She kept thinking what a nice person Laurel was, and what an interesting morning it had been. At the same time, Laurel was having similar thoughts about Kim and the events that had occurred. With a renewed feeling of exhilaration, she headed for her job too. Neither Laurel, nor Kim realized what changes would lay ahead because of this chance meeting.

Kim and Laurel continued to run in the park, and would meet there several times a week. They were becoming friends, and they decided to do a few other things together. One of the first things they did together was to have lunch at the River Boat Cafe. It was anchored by the side of the river just below the Great St. Louis Arch. It became their favorite place. The food there was terrific. All kinds of seafood, and usually the "catch of the day" was on the menu.

Many times after lunch they would walk along the river and watch the boats go by laughing and giggling like a couple of school chums. On their days off from work they would ride the boats down the river and watch the city go by, and talk for hours. Laurel had never experienced this kind of true friendship before. Kim had recently broken up with her boyfriend of two years, and didn't have many friends whose company she enjoyed as much as she enjoyed Laurel's. The friendship had helped to keep her mind off the sadness, even though the breakup had been a good thing, they had grown apart in their relationship.

As time went by, Kim and Laurel found they had lots of similar likes and dislikes. That was what prompted Kim to finally approach Laurel about a partnership in a store she had been thinking about.

"I've been working on a plan to open a store of my own," Kim, began. "I've been doing a lot of thinking about this, and my father is backing me up. Of course, he won't be involved in the planning, or anything like that, but he will be there for any advice I might need. And, one of the things I need is a partner. I've been wondering if you would be interested in a venture like this. I know this is sudden, but I've been thinking about this for a long time. Until now, I just haven't been able to find anyone with whom I felt had the character and integrity to share this kind of deal. That is, until I met you. What do you think? Would you be willing to go into something like this with me?"

"I really appreciate your confidence in me," Laurel said, "and that you think I'm the kind of person you're looking for, but I have to consider all aspects. And, as trivial as it may seem, I'm a little concerned about what might happen to a partnership if either of us decided to get married? You told me you had no plans for marriage in the near future when we talked, but I feel I must protect myself, and any investment I might make. I've been on my own for a very long time, and I can't make any rash decisions unless I'm sure everything is pretty fail-safe, if you know what I mean. I'm sure you must have thought about the same thing. I have to admit, it sounds very tempting, but this has caught me a little off guard. I'll have to think about it." Even though she didn't want to rush into anything, she was very excited about this offer.

"We don't have to make a rush decision here," Kim said, "and if we go ahead with it we can make an iron clad contract that will protect each of us should that occur." At the present time, neither of them had any attachments. With Kim's recent break up, she was not ready to get involved with anyone new right away. She wanted to "find" herself, and see if she could make it on her own in the business world. Laurel, on the other hand, was looking for someone, and if an attractive young man came her way, she would have been delighted. She had always felt the need to have someone to love, and share her life with. She was lonely.

It took awhile, but Laurel thought out every aspect of this venture and had decided to go along with Kim. She could hardly contain her excitement for such a grand idea.

"If this partnership is going to work, the first thing we'll have to do is to make out a plan of exactly what we want to do," Laurel said with enthusiasm. After many meetings, and studying what the area needed most, they decided that it should be an "elite" exotic treasure shop.

"With Dad's help we can set up the business end of this deal, and we can get the company lawyer to finalize the papers," Kim said. A business contract was drawn up, and they were on their way. Laurel had saved money for years, and wanted to invest it in a future. This seemed to be just what she was looking for. She had been a Postmaster in Chicago, and was transferred to a location in St. Louis, one month prior to her chance meeting with Kim.

Being transferred was a godsend, but she had not known it at the time. She had not asked to be transferred, and she was unsure of her future. Now, she thought, *This could be an opportunity to have something of my own, to work for myself.* She realized that it was risky doing business with someone she didn't know all that well, but Kim seemed to be a very honest person. Kim's family had been in the business for two generations. Laurel thought there probably couldn't have been a better time, or a better person for this investment.

At first, Laurel and Kim agreed that Laurel should keep her job at the Post Office. Kim would work at the shop full time. After awhile they could see that the shop was going to be a tremendous success, and Laurel left her job behind. It had been three years since they opened, and they were doing quite well. However, Kim thought they ought to spice things up a bit with a few unique items from other countries. Their store was more for the wealthy shopper than for the average person. There wasn't a piece in their shop that sold for under $500. Laurel was a little apprehensive about the prices, at first, but the market was there.

"People like nice things, and some, don't care what the cost, so we might as well be the ones benefiting from their extravagances," Kim would say. The market was there, and *they* were there to take advantage of an opportunity. An opportunity that was making them rich. They had talked about going to Greece for their first trip, mostly as a pleasure trip with a little business on the side, although no actual plans had been made. They needed to talk over all their options. They could have just talked about it at the store, but this first trip was very important to them.

"This is going to be a turning point in our business strategies. Let's have lunch at our favorite place," Kim suggested. And that place was where they had planned the store originally, the River Boat Cafe. They were both looking forward to this experience.

They alternated days off, and it was Laurel's day off. She told Kim she had something special to show her, and would meet her for lunch at 2 o'clock. Kim put a closed sign on the door of the shop for a couple of hours so they could meet in pleasant surroundings and talk uninterrupted to discuss their plans. She didn't like closing the store during business hours, but for this occasion, she decided to make an exception. Their customers usually knew what they were looking for when they came to shop. She was sure they would return again when they reopened in a couple of hours, but just to be on the safe side, she left a note attached to the closed sign saying when she would be back.

Laurel really enjoyed traveling, and was excited to be going to a foreign country. Kim thought she would have to convince Laurel to go on this trip, but she didn't know how much Laurel really wanted to go, or how glad she was that Kim had suggested the trip. This luncheon meeting, as far as Laurel was concerned, was just to go over a few details about the trip, and to make a list of the things they should see and do while they were in Greece. Laurel practically had her bags packed, even though the trip was still unscheduled. Kim would have an easy time convincing her friend about the value of the trip. Laurel had to laugh at that. She thought she would give Kim a hard time for a few minutes, and act as if she really had to be convinced to go, when in reality she could hardly wait. When Laurel left her apartment she called Kim, but Kim hadn't answered the call. Laurel left a voice message:

"Hi! Kim, Just thought I'd let you know I'm leaving the house right now," Laurel said into the phone. "I may be a little late. Traffic is a heavier than I expected. I realize I should have left earlier, but it's too late now. Sorry for the inconvenience. See you when I get there."

Laurel was actually more adventurous than Kim could ever have imagined. She was, perhaps, showing Kim a more reserved personality that was not the real Laurel. In the three years since they had met, Laurel had not really let her hair down around Kim. Deep down, Laurel was aching for some real excitement in her life. What lay ahead might be more excitement than she had anticipated, and much more than she could ever have imagined.

# CHAPTER THREE

Laurel's life as a child was not happy, as she remembered it, but not necessarily unhappy. Being raised in an orphanage had not been a good situation for her, as it is not for most children. She was brought to this particular orphanage, an ominous three-story building in the plains of eastern Oregon, when she was three years old. The place was located in a desolate area about a mile from civilization. Nothing around it made it seem inviting, and an unexplained loneliness hovered in its hallways and rooms. Her only memory of that day was that someone she could only remember as an elderly gray haired person had left her in this place. She had cried and cried for this person not to leave her. Her sadness lingered until one day she forgot why she was crying, and she stopped. It was almost as if one personality got lost, and a new one appeared, stepping into a world of reality.

No one was coming to take her back home so her young mind had no choice but to move on and to forget. When a person is very young, as she was, forgetting comes naturally, and with it comes a form of numbness, which accompanied her throughout most of the rest of her life. Whoever this person was who left her with such callousness would not register in her childhood memories, thus putting aside the natural need for hatred of any particular person. She had many unanswered questions about who this person might have been, but she sensed that this person had not been her mother.

Laurel never knew who left her that day, and as she grew older, she didn't think she cared. The person, who left her, was her maternal grandmother who felt she had no other choice but to give her away. Laurel's grandfather had been a self-ordained preacher who tolerated nothing that didn't follow his religious beliefs. His daughter had strayed from the holy word, and had gotten pregnant when she was 17. He hid her away during the pregnancy and when the child was born, he hid her too.

Laurel's mother lay sick and unconscious for days before she died because he would not call a doctor. He was a cruel, evil man and his idea of God's will was out of control. He would beat his wife into submission, and he had tried to do the same to his daughter. The old man had never beaten Laurel, but her grandmother thought it was just a matter of time. Her only recourse was to get Laurel away from him before he destroyed her, as he had destroyed his own daughter.

Laurel's grandmother never went to visit her. She was afraid her husband would find out where she had taken her, Shortly after leaving her in the orphanage, they moved away from Oregon and never returned. Her grandmother died, grieving for both her daughter, and granddaughter. Laurel's grandfather didn't grieve for his daughter because in his mind, he had no daughter. She had disobeyed the word of God, as he saw it in his crippled mind, so he would not recognize Laurel as his granddaughter. He lived only a few years longer within his religious fanaticism, thinking God would take care of him, and he did. During a flu epidemic, he died, and the world was a better place.

Laurel was a quiet child, never causing anyone any real grief although, she was a little feisty with her Superiors, sometimes. She had a few friends, but none stayed long enough to become lasting relationships. Just when she would become friends with someone they would be adopted, and she would lose contact with them. She cried herself to sleep wondering why she was never adopted. She thought she might be pretty, but she wasn't sure if she really was. She tried to be friendly when the people came to gaze upon the children, but no one seemed to want her. It may have been the downcast eyes and sullen looks that turned people away. For whatever reason it may have been, they made her feel unworthy, and she always had this feeling of being lost and alone. Rather than causing her to feel sorry for herself though, this made her stronger. She finally decided that there must be a reason for her life to be this way, and maybe someday she would find it.

Once she had resigned herself to being un-adoptable, her life became a semblance of happiness under the circumstances. She would say, "I'll make my own life when I'm old enough to leave this place."

As soon as she was 17 Laurel left the orphanage, and went to California with the little bit of money she had managed to save from the pittance she was paid to clean the offices at the orphanage. Stubborn as she was, and afraid that if anyone knew what she was planning they would try to stop her, since she was still under aged, she walked the mile into town hopped on a bus and left. It was the first time in her life she actually felt free. Living in the orphanage had seemed like living in a prison only she didn't get visitation rights. No one had ever come to visit her. She felt only a little apprehensive about leaving, but she knew she had no choice if she were to start a new life. She would have to get a job right away. Her life hadn't been easy, and she didn't expect that to change. She had accepted her fate and knew she would have to work for everything she would ever have.

One of the first jobs she had was working nights in an apple cannery where they made applesauce. She was put outside in the dark sorting rotten apples from the good ones. Later she moved inside where she folded cardboard shipping boxes. Eventually she advanced to working on an apple-peeling machine. With each advancement, her wages increased. This was not exactly a great job, but it paid the bills. She found a boarding house to live in that was fairly close to where she worked. She could walk there and to most everything else she needed. The woman that ran the boarding house was very kind, and she convinced Laurel to further her education. She helped her apply for Federal grants to pay for her college tuition and some living expenses. It took some time, and a lot of hard work, but she got a good education.

When she applied for the job as Postmaster in Chicago and got it, she felt like she had paid her dues, and was on her way. A new place, a new job, a new life. Then after a few years, she was transferred to St. Louis, and at that time, she wasn't sure what her future might hold. At first, she was angry and apprehensive about this move until she met Kim, and then everything started to change. Her life was finally coming together. She was actually happy, really happy, for the first time in her life.

Kim offered Laurel stability. Having family relationships as Kim had was completely foreign to Laurel, but was something she longed for in a way that most people would not understand. Kim was the closest thing to being family that Laurel had ever known, and she treasured the relationship. Now, if she could find a man to love and share her life with she thought her life would be complete.

# CHAPTER FOUR

Nora busied herself around the counter in the cafe. Washing everything that might need cleaning, but really didn't. Everything was spotless. This was a way of keeping her mind off more pressing matters, mainly the new girl that had just arrived. Although, she never mentioned it to anyone, she was becoming more and more alarmed at what was going on. The secrecy of it all haunted her more each day. *Why couldn't they just tell them what was going on?* she thought. She knew they would tell them eventually, but she thought it should be sooner, *before they were so scared and unsure of themselves.* Well, that was not for her to decide. Her Superiors must have a reason for what they were doing.

Ed was sitting at one of the booths, reading the newspaper. A cup of coffee sat in front of him on the table. Nora had been married to Ed for the past ten years, and not a day went by that she didn't wonder why she stayed. Not that she had many options. At 43 what would she do? Not that she was old, but it was a little too late to start a new life. Where would or could she go? It wasn't that she didn't care for Ed, she just didn't love him. It was just that at times she thought she could have done better with her life had she had the opportunity.

At one time, she had been quite a beauty, but after years of badly abusing her body with drugs and alcohol, she looked worn and tired. Her once black hair was almost totally gray, and her 5' 4 frame carried more weight than it should have. She was still attractive in a way, but more importantly, she was truly a good person. Deep down in her heart was a person who really cared about people.

Nora had lived quite a wild life as a teenager, and it had taken its toll on her. She had never had a formal education, but she was no dummy. As a matter-of-fact, she had been what they call, "street smart." The events that happened in her life had made her that way, but her past finally caught up with her. She became pregnant out of wedlock, and had developed Toxemia. It wasn't taken care of, and she became so sick that she had a severe stroke.

Her life was changed forever after that. She assumed that the baby must have died, because she never saw it. She never knew if it had been a boy or a girl. At the time, she didn't care. The next thing she knew she was brought here, to this place. She had very little memory of any of her past now. It was just a vague thought now and then. She lived a relatively quiet life here in this little town.

Shortly, after she arrived here, they came to her and said she could leave if she wanted to, but she chose to stay, because she had no place else to go. She had no family that she was aware of who would care where she was. This was as good a place as any. She had her health back, and she was happy most of the time. That was good enough for her.

Nora had been put in this position as proprietor just before she met Ed. They came to her one day and said she was needed in this position, she was never quite sure who "they" were, but she didn't question it. How could she have refused? Her attitude was, if you can help someone out, why not do your best. She felt she had to make amends for her past in some way. Although, she wasn't sure why she should care. It was just some underlying feeling that would pass by her mind on occasion.

Someone else had been here at the cafe before her. She hadn't been told where the other proprietors had gone. No explanation had been given. Those people had left the place in good condition, but there was too much work for Nora to do alone. Then "they" the powers that be, some entity unknown to her, sent Ed to her. She never questioned them, she just accepted the assistance he was willing to give. He was supposed to help her with the heavy lifting, and the hard tasks of the job. Most of the regular, mundane jobs, she was required to do by herself.

After being together everyday for quite awhile, Nora and Ed decided to marry. No children had ever come from their union. She thought it was best for both of them, especially after her distant memories of that first pregnancy. She was sure she didn't ever want to go through that again. She thought she might have been too old anyway. Although, she thought she might have made a fine mother, but what could she have done with children in this situation? Too many unknowns. She knew there were plenty of children waiting for homes, but not this one.

Nora walked over to Ed, and offered to fill his coffee cup. He nodded, but hardly looked up from his paper. He didn't seem to pay much attention to anything she did. Whether it was with the people who came through here, or what she did around the cafe.

*Well*, she thought, *Things could be worse*. At least, she was busy and had a roof over her head. Somehow, she just wanted to know that she was needed, and loved. *Was, what she was doing, worthwhile?* she would ask herself. She felt a little guilty for feeling this way. *If you're put in a position for a reason, and prove to be good at what you do, maybe that's what it's all about,* she thought. Perhaps it's against higher laws to reject what you are expected to do.

Anyway, she would continue doing her job until told otherwise by those in higher positions. She sighed and walked into the kitchen to begin preparing the dinner special. She was an especially good cook, and maybe it made things a little easier for those who stopped by to get through their days ahead, which she knew would be a trial for each and everyone of them.

Laurel found the bathroom, and just as Nora had said, there was everything she would need. It was almost as if she had been expected. There was a towel and washcloth, lotions, shampoo, and even makeup. There was a hair dryer and curling iron too.

*Things weren't this organized at home*, she reflected. A shower was going to feel great after what she had been through. She reached for the faucets to the shower, turned the water on, and adjusted the temperature. She wanted it to be nice and hot so she let it run for a few minutes while she unbuttoned her blouse partially and pulled it over her head. She unzipped her pants and stepped out of them. She leaned over to check the water and then, slipped out of her panties and bra letting them fall to the floor. She stepped over the side of the tub and into the spraying water. She closed her eyes and let the water run over her face and down her aching body. *Soon,* she thought, *this nightmare will be over, and I can get back to my life.* She sighed deeply, hoping she was right.

Laurel turned off the water, and reached around for the towel. She towel dried her hair, and then wrapped the towel around her body, hooking it with a tuck. She walked over to the bathroom sink. Looking into the mirror, she ran her fingers through her still wet hair, and inspected the area around the sink with it's "near perfectness." To have everything she needed right here in front of her seemed surreal. Right down to the toothbrush and toothpaste. *This is like "The Twilight Zone,"* she thought and then, almost laughed, but everything was so bazaar that it was hardly a laughing matter. Just then, Nora knocked on the door. "Laurel!" Nora called out. Laurel opened the door slightly.

"Yes, what is it?" she asked timidly.

"I've brought some nice clean clothes for you to put on. Yours looked a little messed up, and here is some juice. It'll make you feel better. Get dressed. Then we'll talk." Laurel did as she was told, and noticed that the clothes were not only clean, but new as well. She put on the clothes, and noted, a perfect fit! Laurel was a size six, and had not always found it easy to find clothes that didn't need some alterations, and yet, these clothes, a pair of faded jeans and a green pullover sweater were perfect. Shoes and a pair of Reeboks also, a perfect fit.

She dressed, and then finished the juice. An odd feeling came over her just as the last of the juice was running down her throat. She left the bathroom feeling very weak, and began walking toward the couch in the outer room. Before she reached it, she lost control of her legs and fell to the floor. Trying to get up, she found herself almost crawling with a heaviness that defied explanation. She tried to hoist herself up onto the couch, but to no avail. She wasn't sure if she had made it onto the couch, because in the next few moments everything slipped away into total, consuming darkness, again. Only, this time, something unnatural had caused her to completely lose control of her body and mind.

29

# CHAPTER FIVE

Ed, Nora's husband, was scary. He had dark hair, and eyes that pierced through you like a knife to your soul. He sulked around most of the time. He appeared to be quiet and unassuming, but underneath, there lay something sinister that no one, not even Ed, knew would come out one day. He was brought to Nora's cafe one afternoon, just shortly after she had taken it over. She needed help and there he was. Nora had to admit that he was pretty good help. Ed was surly sometimes, or it appeared so, because he didn't want to interact with anyone. Just did his job and didn't want to be bothered with anything, or anybody when he had finished. He sat at the table reading the paper while Nora tended to the new one.

He would glance around the paper once in awhile just to see if there was anything he might need to help Nora with, or just to peer at a pretty young girl whenever he had the chance. He wore one of his T-shirt sleeves rolled up like he had a pack of cigarettes tucked in it, but no smoking was allowed. Old habits are hard to change. His jeans were rolled at the cuff too. A holdover from his teenage years. He was 49, but looked 60. His face was wrinkled and transparent from all the smoking he had done throughout his life.

Nora married Ed because she thought she should. Since they were living here together, it did look better. Although, Ed wouldn't have cared one way or the other. He didn't need to impress anyone, but he had to admit he did kind of like having Nora around. She was a good cook, and not too bad in bed. Sometimes, he even thought he might love her, but what did he know about love.

His life hadn't been a bed of roses. He couldn't even remember his parents. He had been on his own for so long, alone, and Nora was the only family he had. When they, that entity that seemed to have power over everyone here, told him that he must come to the cafe to help Nora out, he thought it was an "OK" place. Just biding his time until something better came along. Only this place had a few perks.

30

He thought, *A good cook, and a woman to share my bed. Not too shabby! So what if I had to marry her? It could be worse.* Much worse, but he didn't want to think about that.

Before Ed came to stay at Nora's he had been kind of "out of it." He had been wiped out on drugs more than a few times. The heinous crimes he committed were far beyond any normal person's comprehension. He had been committed to a hospital by the State for rehabilitation after he was found completely out of his mind on drugs, ranting and raving, in the streets of New York. Clever as he was, one day he saw an opportunity to leave, and he just walked away without a hitch. No one even saw him go.

He was just beginning to feel the freedom and the urge to find another victim, when an untimely accident nearly took his life. He was shot in the head in a drive-by shooting. He was at the wrong place at the right time. The bullet lodged in his brain. The shooter was after someone else. How ironic that a stray bullet would change the course of his life. Because, had that bullet not stopped him, he would have gone on raping and killing women for as long as he had a breath in his body.

Ed was born bad, like a bad seed. He was bad because he wanted to be bad. Perhaps, under different circumstances Ed could have been normal. Society would probably blame his parents for his behavior, but in reality what he was, was what he had created in himself. His parents had little to do with what he had become. Their only fault was in being the vessels from which he was produced. He was like the Devil himself. Rehabilitation had not worked for him because he didn't want to change. He liked what he was doing.

He was being good here for the first time in his life. At least now, he was clean. Well, actually, he didn't have a choice. Drugs were not available to him since coming here. He didn't miss them, and he had wondered about that because before, when he had tried to quit he had never been able to kick the habit.

Things were different here, and there was no doubt about that. Ed had noticed that Nora had even been aware that things were "different" here too. There wasn't any other way to express what happened around here. People coming and going at all times of the day and night. Usually, they seemed lost, as lost as this latest girl, Laurel, had been. The people just appeared, apparently from nowhere. Nora would take care of them for a couple of days, and then they are mysteriously removed. Ed vowed that someday soon he was going to find out where they go. He was aware of the reason he was here, he had no choice, but he wasn't sure why Nora was here. He knew it had something to do with all the people she helped, but he thought there must be a greater reason.

Ed and Nora didn't talk much. Ed never saw much use in talking. Even so, evil thoughts were always lingering in his mind. He wasn't sure where these thoughts came from, but that didn't matter. He liked the feelings they gave him anyway. These thoughts were hard to hold onto. When he went outside of the building, an unusual feeling would cause those terrible thoughts to almost vaporize. If he tried really hard, he could still keep a vague idea of evil in the back of his mind. It took lots of concentration, and some days it was too much work, and he would just sit around waiting for Nora to tell him what to do next.

# CHAPTER SIX

Laurel awoke with a start. She was lying on a metal table completely nude with a white sheet draped over her. The last thing she remembered was trying to reach the couch at the cafe before she fell to the floor unconscious. She thought, *There must have been something in that juice Nora gave me.* Now, she was here on this table with smells of Ether and disinfectant permeating the room. She felt like she was in a morgue. As she sat up clutching the sheet to her chest, she looked around the room feeling cold and alone. Nothing could have prepared her for the sense of desperation she was experiencing at this moment. She could see her clothes hanging on a rack across the room.

On the left side of the room, there were metal double swinging doors. The rest of the room looked like a hospital emergency room. Just as she slid off the table, a man in a white lab coat burst through the swinging doors. He had a very arrogant attitude that couldn't be missed. He was very attractive in a strange sort of way. His hair was sandy brown, with red highlights, and he appeared to be in his late twenties or early thirties.

"Oh! You're awake," he said pleasantly, "Good, now we can get on with your examination."

"What examination?" Laurel exclaimed. In her state of mind, it was amazing that she could even offer such a question, that she could even correlate the thoughts to suggest a question was a miracle, but they just seemed to roll out of her mind as if she were actually in control of them.

"It's just a routine examination that we give all the people who come here before we can release them."

"I don't need any kind of examination. I'm just fine, and if you don't mind, I would like to put my clothes on and go home."

"I'm afraid you can't do that just yet, I can't release you until we have given you a complete examination, and a clean bill of health.

We can't let *you people* run around possibly infecting others with whatever diseases you might have brought with you."

"What do you mean, 'You People'?" Laurel asked.

"Well, I shouldn't have said it quite that way…" he paused as if searching for words.

"Well, *you did!* Now *you* can explain to me what you are talking about," Laurel insisted. Laurel could see she wasn't getting anywhere with this doctor, or whatever he was. She moved away from the table, suddenly very much aware that all that was between her and this *person* was the sheet that she was so desperately clinging to.

"May I at least get dressed?"

"No, I'm not finished examining you."

"Oh, yes you are!" Laurel insisted.

"Alright, if you're not going to cooperate with me…Guards!" he yelled. Laurel stood there shocked beyond belief, as two men in white uniforms hurried into the room and grabbed her by her upper arms. Laurel, still clinging to the sheet, started to tremble.

"We have two ways to do this," he said, "the easy way with you cooperating and letting me finished the examination, or the hard way, which will be uncomfortable for you, but easier for me since I'll have to sedate you." Laurel thought she saw a glint of pleasure in his eyes, dark eyes that showed very little emotion. She tried to struggle to loosen the grip of the two guards. She could see that wasn't going to work.

"Okay, make these brutes let go of me!"

"You're sure you will cooperate now?"

"Okay! Okay!" she said rather indignantly, as she raised her hands to ward them off.

"Release her," he said to the guards, and he looked away for a second toward a table of supplies he was planning to use. Laurel pulled the sheet around her back, and across the front of her breasts, tucking it in under her left arm to hold it in place. In an instant, she saw an opportunity to escape. She ducked down and bolted toward the double doors, knocking down everything in her path. Metal

34

tables full of needles and supplies went clanking to the floor causing a terrible commotion. The doctor fell against the patient table as she pushed him out of her way in her desperate attempt to flee. The guards ran after her tripping over everything she had pushed, or shoved out of her way. She had no idea where she was going, or what she was doing, especially since all she was wearing was a sheet, but at least she wasn't going to stay here and be someone's guinea pig, *unless* there were *no way out....*

# CHAPTER SEVEN

Charles was frustrated with what had just happened. He had never had a patient knock him out of the way, and run out of the room the way that Laurel had just done. It was his responsibility to examine all the new ones to make sure they had no diseases that they could pass on to other people while they were here. A death to a physical body from the real world, caused by a disease contracted here, was unacceptable. Cuts and bruises or broken bones never pass through *The Veil*, but diseases do. It had something to do with the diseases being inside the patients' bodies at the time of the pass. Physical impairments were automatically healed as soon as they entered *The Veil*.

Charles would be called on the carpet for losing this one today if he didn't get this under control. He was Dr. Charles Statten, a doctor with an impeccable reputation, and in his mind, there was no room for error. Everyone counted on him to be completely flawless, and he intended to keep it that way.

Charles had been born in this place. Being here was the only life he had known during his 31 years of existence. He had grown up with a nanny, hardly knowing his parents. They left when he was very young. His mother was the first to leave. He remembered her trying to stay, but something kept trying to pull her away. He remembered the headaches she would have. She mentioned that at the time of the headaches she could hear voices too. His mother tried not to leave, but she was not strong enough to stay. Then his father left without a word. He never saw either of them again. He never understood why, and with all the understanding that he had gleaned with maturity, he still had not forgiven them for leaving. Though he missed his parents, his life had been full of love.

When Charles' parents left, he was placed with the nanny who raised him, and she treated him much the same as his mother had. Although, he felt she loved him, and she never left his side, he had always felt alone and abandoned. He had never been able to shake that feeling. Even though, the nanny had explained to him why his parents had to leave, that it had nothing to do with him, and they had loved him. She told him they wanted to stay with him, but a stronger force helped to make their decisions for them.

Whatever was on the other side, in the real world where Charles' parents had come from, must have been very important for them to make the decision to go back through *The Veil* and leave him behind. The other side was where they were meant to live out their lives. It was their "life force plan" that The Creator has for everyone before they are born. Charles being born was not planned, and there was no way for his parents to take him with them. He would not have survived the pass, and he could not have been sustained in their world. Unknown to him, the thought of leaving him here was the most heart wrenching decision they would ever make in their entire lives, but after they passed back through *The Veil* they forgot him and never remembered his existence. He would have to live out his life on this side of *The Veil* in *The Keeping Place*.

Charles became a doctor through no choice of his own. When a person is part of this side they do what is expected of them. All who are born here become Guardians. They are placed where they are best suited to be. Knowledge is a given. Whatever a person is meant to be is automatically in his or her brain. All the knowledge needed for that subject is theirs at birth. They can live a very normal life with all the amenities of living anywhere. Except that, they are expected to be tested to determine the extent of their knowledge at the age of 12. Then, they are readied for their chosen profession for the next few years, until they fully understand their abilities and responsibilities. Therefore, when Charles was tested, it was decided that he had all the knowledge needed to be a doctor. His parents had been very intelligent people. Their union had produced an excellent specimen. He was highly valued among his peers, and those of higher authority.

Charles was careful while growing up never to befriend the ones who passed through from the other side. They were known as the "Spanners," because they had "spanned *The Veil*." Then, there were the "Stayers." Those who chose to stay even if they had the opportunity to return to their own world where they had come from. It bothered Charles terribly that his parents had decided to go back. They had a choice of whether to stay or to leave, and they both chose to leave. Of course, his nanny was a Guardian so he knew she would never leave him. In his mind, he thought his parents could have become Stayers as so many others had. Charles was always studying the Stayers for this reason, and yet, he had a dislike for them that he found hard to understand.

Most of the Spanners, when given an opportunity to leave, *would leave*. Someone or something would always pull them back to the other side to their own world. The Stayers, on the other hand, whether they were called back or not, would choose to stay. What would make them want to stay here, and leave whatever they had before in their own world was always a mystery to Charles. Of course, there were compelling reasons to stay, but could they compare to those offered by the real world? Charles often pondered this question. He knew that this question could only be answered within the hidden secrets of the minds of the people involved, and he always questioned their motives.

The only way the Stayers would ever leave *The Keeping Place*, after they had given up their opportunity to go back to the real world, was if their physical body died while it lay in a coma. At that time, they could never go back to the real world, of course, because their body died. If they chose to, they could go on to another world called "Elysian Fields." If they didn't want to move on to Elysian Fields, they could remain here in *The Keeping Place* for eternity. The Guardians were never given that option, because they never left *this* place, *ever*. They were born here, and they stayed here forever, never dying. They would reach a level of maturity, and never get any older. They could not die, but they could be removed if they ever disobeyed the rules. Where they went when they were removed was privileged information, and only a few knew where the disobedient were sent. It was not something anyone ever wanted to discuss, for fear of the wrath of The Creator. It was considered beyond the realm of intelligent conversation, and very few ever dared bring up the subject. Better left alone.

Charles had often wondered what the world on the other side of *The Veil* was really like. He knew more about his own world, and the Spanner's world, than most of the other Guardians, but even so, he felt his knowledge about this subject was sorely lacking in detail. He knew the basics. He was in a position of "need to know" status. And that was all he was allowed to know. He would, however, whenever he could, find out further details from Spanners when he examined them. Sometimes, if he presented the right questions to a Spanner, he or she would divulge information that he found to be very enlightening. Of course, any information he garnered in this way was strictly confidential. He had to tell those who came to him for examinations, in great detail, why they were here, and what they would need to know while they remained here. He also told them what they needed to know about going back through *The Veil*, although some were here such a short time that it was unnecessary to tell them anything at all.

"Guards! Charles shouted, Seal the doors." He sounded very calm, but he was really quite concerned. He didn't want to let on that there was anything wrong. He hadn't had a chance to examine this person as thoroughly as he had planned, and what if she had brought a virus with her. No disease could attack the Guardians. They never had any kind of physical impairments, such as broken bones or debilitating diseases such as Diabetes, heart diseases, liver ailments, etc. Nor did they ever get any of the crippling diseases.

It was imperative that a virus be controlled for a more important reason. If the Spanners who had come through *The Veil*, previously, contracted a virus from a new Spanner, it would kill them. It was Charles' responsibility to see that this never happened while they were in *The Keeping Place*. If it should happen, those people infected would have no chance of returning to the real world as a living entity, and no chance of staying here with eternal life. Their options would be changed forever, and only The Creator would know where they would be placed for their remaining lives.

Only once before, had Charles seen a virus run through the

community of Spanners. The loss was devastating. It was not meant to happen, and he wasn't about to be responsible for it happening again, even though he had nothing to do with that prior incident. As Charles knew, The Creator had his reasons for people to stay here in *The Keeping Place*, and he had sent down a decree saying that he didn't want those reasons interrupted by uncontrolled accidents. The Creator's life plan for everyone did not include room for error.

# CHAPTER EIGHT

After bolting from the examining room, Laurel could see she was in trouble. She still wasn't quite herself yet since the sedative that was in the juice had not completely worn off. Adrenalin was flowing fast in her body. *Think! Think!* She kept saying. *What should I do? Where should I go?* was rapidly running through her mind. She started running down a corridor with doors along each side. She tried first one door, and then another. All the doors seemed to be locked. When she reached the end of the corridor, she could see there was no way out. Coming toward her were the two guards walking slow and deliberate. She knew they had her now, and so did they as they slowly approached her. She sat down on the floor, and started to sob. The two men came up to her and gently lifted her to her feet.

"It's okay," one of them said, "we are not here to hurt you." Laurel looked at him unbelievingly, but could see it would do no good to struggle. They began the slow march back to the examining room. Laurel was more than apprehensive. She felt trapped, and so alone.

Dr. Statten was quietly awaiting Laurel's return. As she re-entered the room with a guard at each side, holding her firmly by the arms, he motioned to them to place her on the examining table.

"Well, I see you've decided to come back and join me," he said sarcastically. "I can understand your apprehension. Your situation is not uncommon, and I know it can be a bit frightening for some." He was sounding more sympathetic than he had earlier.

"What do you mean, some?" she asked, "and, uncommon? This certainly isn't what I would call a common occurrence. I've never had anything like this happen to me before, and I would like some answers, if you don't mind!" she said forcefully, with tears filling her eyes.

"If you will remain calm for a few minutes, and let me finish my examination, I'll tell what is going on, and where you are," he said. Laurel reluctantly agreed to cooperate because she didn't see where she had any choice in the matter. This doctor was determined to examine her, whether she liked it or not. There was nothing at all wrong with her as far as she was concerned, and an examination was an intrusion into her life, but resistance at this point had accomplished nothing. She was no closer to finding out what was going on now than she had been when she first arrived. Cooperating appeared to be the best solution.

After finishing his examination of Laurel, Charles leaned his back against the table by the wall, half sitting, half standing, looking directly across into Laurel's eyes. It made her uncomfortable, and she felt he had acquired a cocky, self-assured attitude since she had decided to cooperate. She averted her eyes, but then he began to speak, and she immediately looked back at him eagerly awaiting the answers he had promised.

"Alright, here it is," he said. "I'll start from the beginning."

"By all means," Laurel said with disdain. "That sounds like as good a place as any." She had a hard time controlling her anger. She seemed to be more able to hold onto her sanity by being angry. She felt that if she let go of her anger, she might not be able to cope with what was happening to her. This was so far from any comprehension on her part that even anger might not help her keep it together, but she was trying very hard.

"Do you remember leaving your house this morning?"

"Of course, I do. Why wouldn't I?"

"Calm down, if you will just listen I'll tell you what has happened since you left your home today." Laurel decided she might as well listen to what he had to say, as she gathered the sheet more tightly around herself.

"Perhaps you would feel better about what I'm going to tell you if you were dressed. Your clothes are on that rack, and you can dress over there," he said, as he pointed to a screen in a corner of the room. Laurel carefully slipped off the table still warily looking at Charles and holding tightly to the sheet with both hands as she walked over to where her clothes were hanging on the rack. She reached up with one hand, pulled her clothes off the rack and stepped behind the screen. A few minutes later, she immerged from behind the screen, fully dressed in the sweater and pants that Nora had given her.

He waited for her to cross the room toward him and he said, "Please sit down."

She hesitated for a moment, and said, "I'm okay standing."

"No, I think you had better sit down because what I am about to tell you will, no doubt, shock you, and you may be safer sitting." Laurel walked slowly to the chair at end of the examining table, while looking at the doctor suspiciously. She had a puzzled look on her face, as if she were about to speak, but said nothing. She sat in the chair, and pulled her knees up under her chin, wrapping her arms around them tightly, trying to withdraw within herself. Then, she waited for the doctor to begin.

"What I'm about to tell you may seem unbelievable, but is in reality, very true. You are in a transcendental area called *The Keeping Place*. It's a holding sector for people. A place for them to stay while they are recovering from a coma." Laurel grasped the arms of the chair. Her mouth fell open, and she started to rise out of the chair.

"This is impossible. I've never been in a coma. There must be some kind of mistake."

"No, there has been no mistake. There is only one way you can get here, and that is by slipping into a coma."

Laurel fell back into the chair. Her mind was whirling around thoughts that were incomprehensible. "How is this possible!" she exclaimed.

"From what I am to understand, you left your home this morning, and while driving your car you were in a near fatal car accident. Actually, you are lucky to be alive.

"Am I alive?" she asked. "This doesn't exactly look like I lived through it."

"Well, you did, and here you are," he said assuredly.

She sat there for a long few minutes, thinking, letting it all sink in. "What happens now?" she asked questioning his every word, still not totally believing what he had said. She kept thinking that maybe she had been kidnapped or maybe, all this was a terrible hoax, a game, some cruel joke that someone was playing on her. *This couldn't be real, it just couldn't be!* She thought. The sound of his voice brought her back from her thoughts.

"Whether you leave this place, or stay depends entirely on you," he said rather sternly. "It won't do you any good to fight this situation. You're here, and you might just as well deal with it the best you can. You are not the first person to have this happen, and no doubt, will not be the last. Surely, you must know of people who have been in comas. What do you think happens to them?"

She stuttered for a moment, and said, "I...I...guess," she paused. "I never gave it much thought before. I thought they just laid there until they woke up or...died," she said bluntly.

"They don't. The Creator won't allow that to happen."

"What do you mean, 'The Creator'?"

"The 'Creator' is the force that controls our world. I understand that in your world, people call such a person, God. Although, we have much more contact with this being than you do in your world. We have evolved past your primal level. We're here to take care of you during your stay, and we are called, 'The Guardians'. When I say 'we', I mean any of the people you have had, and will have, contact with who are workers here. We live here and cannot leave. It is our only purpose for being. If it were not for people like you, in situations like this, we would not exist. This may be hard for you to understand, especially in your agitated state of mind. There are some things that defy understanding. Things that are far too advanced for the human mind to comprehend. I am only telling you this because it may make your stay easier."

"Easier? How...can you...in your right mind...think that anything...you have told me today...would make any of this easier? This is the most bizarre thing I have ever heard of...and I'm having...a hard time believing...that you are telling me the truth," she said, gasping for air between her words.

"I know this is hard for you, but you really must calm down." She was starting to hyperventilate. He was afraid she was going to faint from lack of oxygen.

"Please, take some deep breaths, and try to calm yourself."

She dropped her feet to the floor and lowered her head to her knees, and when she regained her composure, she raised her head and asked, "If what you say is true, can I ever leave here?"

"First, your physical body must heal. That's why you're here, for the healing."

As if reality were setting in, she asked almost in a whisper, "What if my body doesn't heal?"

"If that should happen, if your body does not heal, which we do not anticipate," he added, "you can never go back to your world. You will stay here until you are called to another place that I believe you call Heaven. We call it Elysian Fields. You would be able to decide for yourself whether, or not, you wanted to go there. Although, all indications are that your body will heal itself, with time, and you *will* be able to go back."

"Thank God!" she said with a sigh of relief, and she brushed her hair back with both hands and leaned back in the chair.

"When your body does heal, someone from your world can call you back at any time. You must be ready to make your decision if this happens. It seems simple enough, but at this time, no one has called you back. Apparently, your body has not healed enough to allow that."

"What if no one calls me back? What can I do to help myself?"

"In some rare cases a person can have such a desire to go back that he or she can actually will themselves back through *The Veil*. Only *very* strong people have ever been able to do that. I've seen it done, although it is rare and almost impossible.

"Why would anyone want to stay here if they had a choice to go home? Why wouldn't everyone try to will themselves back?" Laurel asked, her thoughts deepening.

"The argument to stay is strong, given that here you would have eternal life, but staying is not recommended," he added. "Here, you can live much the same as you did in your world, with a few exceptions. Choosing to live here gives you immortality, which is usually the greatest reason for people to stay, but why they actually stay is still a mystery to me. What goes on in a person's mind is between him, and whichever force is stronger. Personally, I don't understand it, but it is of no consequence to me. After I have examined you, and you leave my office, with no further need of my services, whatever decisions you make are totally your own. However, I can tell you this, if you were to stay here, as I said before, you would live forever, and you could never be hurt physically again. Some other, more menial things you may notice while you're here are that your senses are more acute. Colors may seem brighter. Taste will be more important to you. Sights and smells will impress you, I am sure…"

"Wait just a minute," Laurel said, raising her hand to stop him, and yet trying not to be rude. "You keep talking about these choices I have. I haven't made a choice to be here!"

"Oh, but you have, however, probably not intentionally. While driving, you chose to make the moves that caused the accident. Those choices put you in harm's way, and those choices have put you here. You live, or you die with the choices you make. We'll probably never know for sure why those choices put you here. The Creator has his reasons. We don't recommend that you stay here. If, or when, your physical body heals," he said. "it may be to your best interest to go back, and it probably is, but we leave that choice up to you. There may be other options in your world that are pertinent to your life plan, and in that case, it would be imperative for you to return. If you need counseling to help you make that decision, a counselor can be made available to you. If, or when, you go back you will have no memory of this place. If you stay here, you will be able to remember your former life. We who live here know many things about your realm, but you and those of your world have no knowledge of ours." He offered this, and paused for a moment waiting for her next response. Laurel said nothing so he went on.

"In the meantime, there are some important things I must tell you about staying here for now. I will need to meet with you several times to be able to give you everything you need to handle this situation.

Right now, I believe you have been given enough information to handle. Too much information too soon is unproductive."

Laurel glanced across the room, confused, trying to put her thoughts together. She didn't quite know what to do, but at least she would cooperate with this man in order to find out everything about this place. Anything, that might help her find a way out of this nightmare, out of this place called *The Keeping Place*.

# CHAPTER NINE

Kim reached into her purse to get her cell phone. It rang several times before she realized it was ringing. She had been waiting for Laurel for 45 minutes. The waiter had been by her table several times, asking if she were ready to order. She was getting rather annoyed, and was sure that this must be Laurel calling to explain why she was late. She had not gotten Laurel's earlier message saying she was just leaving her apartment. Kim couldn't imagine what could be making her so late. *What could possibly be keeping her?* Laurel surely must have had her cell phone with her, and Kim wondered why she hadn't called. This call must be Laurel, she thought, *I'm not waiting much longer, and she had better have a good excuse!* When she picked up the cell phone, she realized there *had* been another call. It had been one from Laurel that she had missed, but it was too late now.

"Hello," she said, as someone came on the line asking her if she were Kim Donalson. "Yes, This is Kim Donalson what can I do for you?" She thought this call, since it wasn't Laurel, must be someone needing something from the store. She was irritated that anyone was bothering her now when she was trying to be mad at Laurel.

The woman on the other end of the line said, "I'm Sarah Wells, and I'm calling you from the Downtown Hospital. We're sorry to inform you that a friend of yours, a Laurel Richards, has been in an accident. She is in critical condition, and we need someone here immediately to make some decisions." Kim didn't know what to think. She couldn't find the words.

Not believing what she was hearing she said, "There must be some kind of mistake. You must have made a mistake, it can't be Laurel."

"No, this is not a mistake. I'm sorry to have to tell you this, but the identification in her purse shows Laurel Richards as her name. We need you here right away."

"Ya, Yes, I'll be right there, I'm on my way." She shoved her phone into her purse, and she darted out of the restaurant, slamming the door behind her. For a moment, she couldn't even remember where she had parked her car. Then she saw it and ran to it as fast as she could. She fumbled with her keys to unlock the car door, and after several seconds, she dropped them to the pavement. She reached down to retrieve them, and when she finally got the car door open, she sat down on the seat with a feeling of exasperation. It seemed as if she were moving in slow motion. She leaned back in the seat for a second trying to clear her head. Her hands were shaking. She thought, *I must calm down or I won't be of any help to Laurel, or anyone else.*

Kim was trying to make sense of all this, but all she could think of was that *she* was all Laurel had. Laurel had never known her parents, and she had been raised in an orphanage for most of her life. She may have had some distant relatives, but none that she ever talked about. Kim wasn't sure if they existed, or where they might be. If any existed, they had not been close enough, or cared enough to raise her. Kim decided that she must calm down and be the strength that Laurel needed now. She had to, she had no other choice.

Traffic was terrible, and it took longer to reach the hospital than Kim had anticipated, almost 40 minutes. She parked the car and headed toward the hospital, almost running. She went in through the front doors, and headed straight for the admissions desk. There were nurses standing around the admissions desk. Kim walked quickly up to the first one she could see that she thought would handle new admissions.

"I've come to see Laurel Richards, someone from here called me." she said, her voice trembling.

"What is your relationship to Ms. Richards?" the admissions nurse asked.

"I'm her friend and business partner."

"I'm sorry, the nurse added, only family members are allowed to see a patient in the critical ward."

"But they called me! Someone named Sarah something," Kim insisted. "She has no immediate family. Her parents are dead. She has no one but me!"

The nurse looked at Kim with an uneasiness that frightened her. "I guess if you're her only contact we'll be able to let you see her. Could the person that called you be Sarah Wells?"

"Yes, I think so," Kim said impatiently.

"Hmm, let me see, I believe your friend is still in surgery. Wait here while I do some checking." Kim paced nervously back and forth in front of the Admissions Desk. She couldn't believe they could be so stupid. *They called her, someone here should know something. Surgery…*the very thought of it scared her. She hadn't expected it to be this serious. *The nurse must be wrong,* she thought. In a few minutes, the nurse returned with a person dressed in street clothes. Not the usual white nurses uniform that most of them wear.

She reached out her hand and grasped Kim's limp hand and said, "I'm Sarah Wells. I presume you are Kim Donalson?" Kim nodded her head. "I'm the person who called you. Please follow me." Kim followed as they walked down a hallway to an elevator. Sarah pushed the button for the elevator, and while they waited for it to arrive, she smiled slightly and said, "We have to be very careful who we let in to see patients, especially when they are so critically ill." Sarah took Kim to a waiting room outside the surgery department.

"Your friend has been in surgery ever since she was admitted to the hospital an hour and a half ago. The doctors anticipate at least another hour. She was in pretty bad shape when she came in. She has not regained consciousness. We can only hope that after surgery, she will regain consciousness, and we can at that time, decide what the prognosis is." Kim was in shock. She couldn't find the words to describe what she was feeling. Sarah asked, "Can I get you something? Coffee, maybe?"

"Yes…yes…that would be fine," Kim said without thinking. She sat down on a couch near the door, as Sarah left her to get the coffee. She was only gone for a few minutes when she returned with the hot drink.

Sarah handed it carefully to Kim as she said, "It is very hot. I don't want you to burn yourself." Then Sarah returned to the seriousness of the situation, "The only thing I can tell you about your friend is that we had to take her straight into surgery. There was no time to get permission from anyone. Time was of the essence. It was a life or death situation. As soon as the doctor has finished the surgery, he will come and explain her condition to you. If you will excuse me, I must check on the admission papers and make sure everything is in order. I'll send a nurse to help you fill out some papers. At this time, we don't have much information about her." She left the room leaving Kim alone. All the while, Kim said nothing, still holding the cup of coffee with a steel grip unable to even lift it to her lips.

Another nurse brought the papers in as Sarah said she would, and Kim filled them out the best she could with her limited knowledge of Laurel's previous health conditions. Her actions were very mechanical. She felt like the pen was moving by itself with no connection to her, whatsoever. Whether she had filled out the papers correctly, or not, she hadn't a clue. When left alone again she just stared across the room with a blank look on her face, unable to grasp the situation. It seemed so unreal. Two hours later, Sarah returned to the waiting room, and was surprised to see Kim still waiting there.

Kim actually thought that if she sat still long enough, didn't talk to anyone, maybe, it would all go away. Maybe it really didn't happen, but this person breaking the silence had brought her back to reality.

"Has anyone come to talk to you about your friend?" Sarah asked. "She came out of surgery about a half an hour ago. I thought the doctor would have been here by now to talk to you."

"No...no...I haven't talked to anyone, nor have I been told anything," Kim stated emphatically, coming to her senses.

"I'll take you to the recovery room where she has been taken, and a doctor will be here shortly to talk to you. She has been placed in a private room, as is the case, when someone is in such serious condition. She is being kept in *Room 312*." They took the elevator to the third floor, and as the doors opened, Kim could see signs on the wall stating that they were on the Coma Ward floor. There were directions to the rooms on the walls. Sarah led the way down a long corridor to *Room 312*.

"Why are we on the Coma floor?" Kim asked Sarah.

"Your friend is still under sedation, but her vital signs indicate that she is in a coma. In this hospital, patients are placed where they will be best served for the condition they are in, rather than in a critical ward, that serves every kind of problem. That way patients don't have to be moved again while they are in a state of trauma. The doctors and nurses can watch for specific signs of recovery here that are directly related to her case. Your friend is in good hands here," Sarah said as she gently patted Kim on the back to reassure her. "When your friend regains consciousness, she will be moved."

The door to the room was closed, and when Sarah opened the door, Kim looked across the room at the person in the bed, and nearly fainted. There were tubes connected to Laurel, some in her nose, and one in each arm. One leg was bandaged, and was placed in a sling that hung from the ceiling. Her head was bandaged, and one eye was covered with part of the bandage. Kim's hand flew up to her mouth as she tried to hold in a muffled moan.

All she could say was, "Oh! My God! my God!" and she kept repeating it in a low voice. Tears started pouring down her face. She hadn't expected this. It was much worse than she could ever have imagined. "Oh, Laurel," she cried, "what's happened to you?" In her subconscious mind, she knew Laurel could not reply. The state of shock she was in didn't let her conscious mind seek reason.

Sarah, concerned about Kim's reaction, questioned, "Are you alright? Should I get someone to sit with you?"

At first, Kim said nothing. She was numb, and then, "No, No, I'll be alright in a minute, this is just such a shock. I just cannot believe this. I had no idea."

"Alright then, I'll leave you alone for a few minutes. The doctor will be here soon."

"Thank you," Kim said automatically, without looking at Sarah, still staring in disbelief at Laurel. Left alone in the room Kim leaned over Laurel and said, "Oh, Laurel, I'm so sorry," and she sobbed uncontrollably. She sat back in the chair by the bed that had been provided for visitors, and covered her eyes and cried. She couldn't think what to do. Then, she remembered the other call on her cell phone. She retrieved the call, and listened to the message Laurel had left. She placed it on speaker phone, and she listened to it over and over again.

"Hi! Kim, Just thought I'd let you know I'm leaving the house right now. I may be a little late. Traffic is heavier than I expected. I realize I should have left earlier, but it's too late now. Sorry for the inconvenience. See you when I get there."

The sound echoed in the room in the eerie silence. This broken body in this bed was the same person on the phone who had just a few hours ago been so alive. Kim was overwhelmed with pity and concern, and still in a state of disbelief and total denial even with Laurel's mangled body lying there wrapped in white bandages from head to foot. She wrapped her arms tightly around herself, rocked back and forth, and cried with such a feeling of despair, as she had never known before. This was Laurel, her friend. Lost in pain and sorrow, what could she do for Laurel now when she needed her most? That question hung in her mind as her heart was aching, and along with that pain, she was harboring feelings of terrible guilt for being mad at her friend earlier.

# CHAPTER TEN

Laurel felt overwhelmed with all the information Dr. Statten had given her. She was still having trouble comprehending that what he had told her could actually be true. But, on the other hand, what other explanation could there be. No one would go to the trouble to put together such a tremendous hoax. There would be no reason. She sat there trying to let it all sink in while Dr. Statten walked away from the table for a moment, and began moving instruments around on the counter next to the wall. He said, "Since I have finished your examination you're free to go."

"Where?" Laurel asked.

"Anywhere, you want to go. There is a town here. We have several cafes and clothing stores. Much the same as you would have in your own home town. Although, everything is free. Food, clothing, whatever you feel the need to have. Of course, greed is not tolerated. But there is no need for that, because you can have anything you want at any time. I would suggest that you walk around town to see the place, and then register at one of the hotels for a place to stay while you are here."

Laurel thought, *He keeps referring to "while I stay" here. Like I've come for a vacation. Like I'm in the south of France, and just decided to drop by the doctor's office, and in a week I'll be heading back home. How ludicrous is that?!* Thoughts just came pouring into her mind. Maybe, she was being too critical, and maybe he really did mean that she would be leaving soon. That thought made her feel better, because she had no intention of staying here if there were any way possible to leave. She had reluctantly submitted to the examination, but it was over now and she had made a decision. She decided she would come back to talk to him, as he had suggested, to find out everything she could about this place.

He said, "Start thinking about what you want to do right away, because you must be ready when the time comes to leave." She noticed the emphasis on "must," but she didn't ask him any more questions. She needed to get her bearings, and the only way she could do that was to be released to walk around freely.

When Dr. Statten released her, with an appointment to come back the next day, she left his office and walked out into the corridor. There were no guards in white coats lurking to grab her. She felt apprehensive about leaving, but she kept going down the hall to the double doors that led to an "outside" to somewhere, half expecting to be apprehended at any moment. As she pushed the doors open to the outside, she had a tremendous feeling of relief. Like she had just escaped from whatever seemed to have had a hold on her.

Laurel looked up, and was amazed by the colors all around her. The doctor had been right about colors being brighter, they were actually brilliant. The sky was bluer than she could have ever imagined, and the grass was the greenest grass she had ever seen. Even the gray concrete of the sidewalk looked vibrant. She had never been able to see quite so clearly. She had always worn corrective lenses, and now to be able to see without any aids, such as glasses or contact lenses was absolutely amazing. It was wonderful! She was surprised that she was feeling so well. Although, she still felt scared of what might lay ahead, she was at least willing to move ahead and see what this was all about. Whatever the consequences might be, she was ready. Even though, she had been so upset only a few hours before, she now felt the need to continue with her life, such as it was. For the time being, she would make the best of it.

Laurel walked along the sidewalk enjoying the beautiful colors. Flowering trees lined the streets. She had to admit this was one of the loveliest places she had ever seen. It reminded her of a beautiful painting. In the distance she could see people walking. *That must be where she should go,* she thought. There were buildings along the skyline in very calm cream colors and pastels, all standing neatly in rows. The streets were clean. As a matter of fact, they were spotless. It was like walking the streets of *Disneyland*. There were tables nicely positioned in front of a couple of eating places. She decided to stop in one to get something to drink. Couples were seated around the tables smiling and talking. As she seated herself at one of the little tables that would seat only two people, a waiter walked up to her and asked if he could help her.

"Why, yes, you may." she said. "I would like a...well, what do you have?"

"We have anything that you would like, soft drinks of any flavor, ice tea of any flavor, and water of any flavor, and of course any juices you might like. We don't, however, serve alcoholic beverages."

"What kinds of flavors do waters come in?" she asked quite puzzled.

"You know, that is usually the first question newcomers ask. I guess where you come from water doesn't come in flavors?" he queried, and then began giving her the flavors. "We have River Water, Lake Water, Sky Water, Forest Water, and if you are not very adventurous, Lemon Water. Forest Water is very refreshing."

"Okay, I'll try that." she said with a smile. A few minutes later he brought her the Forest Water she had ordered, and he sat it on the table with a bow and a smile.

"Is there anything else I can get for you?"

"Not at the moment." she said, as she looked around at the seating area. *This is amazing,* she thought. *All these people seem to be very happy. No one is this happy. Something must be wrong. Perhaps these are the Stayers that Dr. Statten had talked about.* It certainly did look like a paradise, but how could you possibly be happy about leaving everything you have ever known, be thrown into another world, and still be happy about it. She would have expected someone to feel the way she was feeling. But then, just how was she feeling? Since she left the doctor's office she was actually feeling pretty well. This would, indeed, need some investigation. She finished her drink, and it was deliciously fresh and unusual tasting. Now, she would find a place to stay for the night.

Another short walk found Laurel in front of a hotel, of sorts, that was only three stories high. The first in a series of hotel establishments that lined the street. She thought she might as well try the first one, and if it didn't suit her needs, she could try the next one. She felt like one of the *Three Little Pigs, this one is made of straw, this one is made of wood, and this one is made of bricks,* she giggled to herself. She thought she would try the one made of bricks. Straw and wood wouldn't fill her need to feel secure right now. Her sarcastic humor seemed to be keeping her together. As she walked through the door to the hotel, she couldn't help but think about the cleanliness of this place. Not just the hotel, but everything around her. She remembered a saying that one of her teacher's used to say when she was a little girl, *Cleanliness is next to Godliness,* and it was certainly so here. At least, the cleanliness part. She wasn't sure about the Godliness, but she would find out before long, she was sure. It was funny that she would remember something like that, since there was little else of any good that she remembered from her childhood.

Laurel walked up to the desk and asked the clerk if she could see a room. He said in a jovial tone, "They're all the same. The only differences are the colors. Tell me, what's your color preference?"

"Alright, let's try purple." she said with that same bit of sarcasm in her voice that seemed to keep coming out of her mouth. *She might as well have purple, why not? Everything else here was so far out she might as well have a purple room.* Her humor even surprised herself, considering the dire circumstances she was in. She followed the clerk up a spiral staircase to the third floor of the hotel. Everything was lovely, even in the hallways. There was flowered wallpaper on all the walls and paintings hung about every three feet. The area around the top of the staircase was like a circular sitting room with couches and chairs positioned around the walls. There was a window at one side of this sitting area that looked out over the city. She stopped for a moment to look out, but then hurried to catch up to the clerk. He stopped in front of *Room Number 312.*

# CHAPTER ELEVEN

Charles couldn't stop thinking about his last patient. She was a pretty girl, maybe 26 or 27. Dark hair and eyes with beautiful soft white skin. She was in perfect health. He was able to release her right after his examination. She was physically in perfect shape too, a person who had obviously taken care of herself. A perfect specimen. He usually didn't pay any attention to his patients, but this one had kept his attention. Maybe, it was her sense of desperation that had made him feel sorry for her, and at the same time he admired her determination. He hadn't been sure if he were going to be able to examine her without restraining her. Most patients were very docile when delivered to him. This had been an interesting afternoon. He looked forward to seeing her again. Perhaps she would decide to stay for awhile, and he would get to know more about her.

Charles was surprised at this reaction in himself, because he rarely, if ever, cared about learning anything about these patients since they didn't usually stay very long. Besides, he usually had other things to occupy his time. Thinking about that, he unbuttoned his white lab coat, and hung it on the rack by the door. After examining Laurel, he had made arrangements to meet with a few friends, and he wanted to see what they thought about this patient. His school friends always liked a challenge when it came to medicine. He and his friends only dealt with viruses. Something new like this should prove to be very interesting conversation for the evening. He wanted to know if any of them had experienced a similar incident.

When Charles walked out of the building it was dark. He loved this time of the evening. The stars were shining brightly, and the sun having gone down made the evening air the perfect temperature for walking. He stopped along the way to get a sandwich at the sidewalk cafe, and he planned to take it to his room and eat before he left for his friends' meeting place. They would usually meet at the park a few blocks from his apartment. The park had a lighted seating area with tables and benches, and it was off limits for Spanners. Only Stayers and Guardians could meet here.

There was an invisible barrier around the perimeter of the park. From all outward appearances it looked like an ordinary open area. People could see into it, but could not enter. The barrier would automatically open for a Guardian or a Stayer wherever they were standing, and they could just walk through the opening that was provided. Charles' apartment, being only a few blocks from the park, was an easy walk. When he finished his dinner he headed in that direction to meet his colleagues. When he approached the park the barrier opened for him and he entered, and walked over to a group of young people sitting at one of the various seating areas in the central part of the park.

It had been several weeks since Charles had seen any of these friends. He was glad for this meeting. "Charles!" Frank exclaimed as he jumped up and walked over to greet his friend. "Good to see you, Man. What's this all about? You seemed excited when you called." Charles and Frank were genuinely glad to see each other.

"Well, I have this patient I want to tell you about, but first, I'd like a cup of coffee." They walked over to the table where their friends were seated. The men all had a similar look. Young professionals with an arrogant air about them, and all exceptionally handsome. Each of them had a different shade of red hair. All except for one who stood out from the rest. Frank introduced Charles to this new person, named Reece, whom Charles had never seen before. Reese had curly blond hair and bright blue eyes. They shook hands, and everyone started talking at once. They all seemed to be in a good mood, laughing and talking about nothing in particular. The regulars were a woman named Mary, also redheaded and very pretty. She too had the same arrogant air about her. The other two men were Bill and Ryan. Frank, Bill, Ryan and Mary were all Guardians. They had gone to school together with Charles. Charles didn't know where this new person had come from. Frank apparently didn't feel the need to explain that at the moment. Charles was concerned about talking professional business with a stranger around. He walked over to the snack bar that stood to one side of the seating area, and ordered his coffee. Frank followed him.

"Frank, what's this new person doing here? Where did he come from?"

"He's alright. He's a Stayer. He was a doctor in his world. He likes it here, and he decided to stay. He's been here a couple of years, I'm surprised you haven't seen him around."

"So am I. I thought I knew just about everyone here, but I guess when you're not looking for someone, you don't see them."

Frank continued without paying much attention to what Charles had said, "It's really interesting to discuss medicine with him. He knows so much. It's fascinating to listen to him talk of all the things he has done."

"Do you think we can trust him?"

"Yeah, I'm sure of it. You don't have to worry about him," Frank said, with a smile on his face.

Reluctantly, Charles smiled, and said, "Okay, if you're sure." Together they strode back to the table where the others were engaged in conversations about various topics. Nothing very important. Mostly trivial things that had happened during their work day. When Frank and Charles sat down, the conversation stopped abruptly, and all eyes turned to Charles. He was very much respected with his peers.

"Let's hear it, Charles." Bill said. "What's this incident you wanted to talk about? Frank said you seemed excited about something." They all seemed interested in what Charles had to say.

"Well, I didn't mean for this to be blown out of proportion."

"I hope you don't think I blew it out of proportion?" Frank said, lightly.

"Oh no, no! I meant by me, Charles said, becoming a little embarrassed at the attention he was getting. "It's probably not even very interesting to you guys. I hope I haven't built up your expectations too much. It's just that I had this unusual patient today. She nearly tore my lab apart trying to escape."

"Escape from what?" laughed Frank. "Are you holding people hostage over there in your lab?" This brought a round of laughter from the group.

"Seriously you guys, it's not as funny as it sounds. As strange as that may seem, I actually think she thought we were holding her against her will. I had to have my assistants chase her down the hall, and bring her back into the lab. They had to hold her until she finally settled down. I thought I was going to have to sedate her. She's a really pretty young woman, dark hair and eyes, probably 26 or 27, and in terrific physical condition. I can attest to that from the way she was able to break away from my assistants, and they are really strong guys."

"Really?" Ryan queried, not really wanting to question his friend, more like disbelief. "She must be a change from the norm. Most of my patients are very docile, but go on. This is getting good!"

"You're right about that," Charles said. "Most of my patients are docile too. But this girl.... She knocked over my instrument trays and shoved me into the examining table before she bolted out of the lab doors, and ran down the hall. Luckily, she didn't find a way out. My assistants brought her back, and then I was able to talk some sense into her. She finally calmed down enough for me to finish my examination, and I explained some of what she should know about being here. I made an appointment for her to come back to see me tomorrow. Since she is coming back tomorrow I didn't tell her everything today. She seemed too distraught and I thought maybe I should ease her into things a little more slowly."

"I don't know for sure, but having your guards restrain a person might be construed by that person as being held against her will, don't you think?" Frank said, teasingly.

Missing the humor in Frank's remark, Charles said, "Well, I don't know how else I could have kept her there. I find some people have a hard time grasping all of this at once. I had to at least tell her a few things before I let her wander off. I can tell her the rest or anything I missed telling her when we meet tomorrow. What puzzled me most, like Ryan said, was that she wasn't docile like most of the other patients that come to me. Have any of you seen that kind of reaction before?" Most of them said, "No" in unison.

Except Bill who said, "I had a case similar to that a few years ago. I don't really understand why. I never said anything to anyone about it. I'm glad you brought this up, because I have to admit I was puzzled too. But, this guy I'm talking about was almost crazy. We couldn't get him to understand anything we were trying to tell him. He's still around here somewhere. He decided to stay and I'll say, that surprised me. Although, I was told he had messed up his life pretty badly in his own world. I think someone said they saw him working in that roadside cafe of Nora's. His name was Ed, something or other."

Reece spoke up, "I don't know why these reactions should shock any of you. I'm surprised you don't have more people like that. What can you expect? They've been ripped from a world, another life, so suddenly and it's scary, I know, I've been there. I know I was docile like most of your other patients outwardly, but inside I was terrified."

"That's a good point, Reece," Mary added. "I guess we're so used to everything here that we aren't aware of those feelings. I never thought about it that way."

"I must say," Charles reflected, "Except for the fact that she tore up my lab, I certainly do admire her tenacity. I am looking forward to seeing her again. I hope she stays long enough for me to talk to her a few more times." The men looked at each other questioningly. Maybe there was more to this than just a puzzling situation?

Reece stood up and said he had to leave, but before he did he walked around to where Charles was sitting and he asked, "When she comes back for her appointment, would you mind if I talked to her? I might be able to help her with the transition, with a little more understanding, I mean…," he paused slightly, "since I've gone through the same things that she is going through now." Reece didn't want to invade anyone else's space, but a patient's needs should come first.

Charles didn't quite know how to take that request, *and yet*, he thought, *it might help*. He didn't want professional jealousy to get in the way of a patient's health so he hesitantly agreed. "Be at my office at 4:00 tomorrow and I'll let you observe. You may be right. It may help her."

Reece said his good byes and left the group. Being new to the group he didn't want to overstay his welcome. Charles was glad he left. Now, he could be more relaxed with his friends. He never liked meeting new people, and he didn't like sharing his friends, especially with a "Stayer." Charles wasn't quite sure what to think of Reece. Maybe, it was just insecurity about meeting someone new, but he wasn't sure he liked him. The jovial attitude had changed to a more serious nature, and after a few minutes everyone decided to leave. They walked together to the entrance of the park. Leaving together, they went their separate ways each telling the other they should meet again soon. Charles had wished they could have spent more time together. When Reece had asked to see Charles' patient, everyone had sensed that it had upset Charles, and it changed the mood of evening. Unknown to Reece, he had unwittingly put his friendship with the group in jeopardy.

# CHAPTER TWELVE

Sarah was concerned that Ms. Donalson might be too upset to be alone. She hurried down the hall to find the doctor who had been administering to Ms. Richards earlier. She didn't want to leave Kim by herself for very long. Although, it was probably alright for her to be alone for a few minutes to pull herself together while getting over the initial shock. However, any longer than that, without further information about her friend, might be harmful to her.

Sarah found the doctor having coffee in the doctor's lounge. It had been a particularly stressful day. James Martin sat with his hands over his eyes with his elbows resting on the table. He looked exhausted, and his Light brown wavy hair had fallen across his forehead. He was the Chief House Physician in charge of ER.

Sarah was almost afraid to bother him, but sensing the urgency of the situation, she said, "Ahem," paused and waited for acknowledgment before she continued. Dr. Martin had been in the emergency room when Laurel was brought in. He was young, in his early thirties, only a few years out of medical school, but so well qualified that he had moved right up the ladder into the position he now held, in this small, but very good hospital. He was working more hours than anyone should have been allowed, but he did what had to be done. When Laurel came in, he operated on her broken body and did everything he could to stabilize her. The damages she sustained to her head were extensive. There was a contusion on the left side of her head. Being very concerned he called in a Neurologist to verify his results.

The second doctor agreed with James' prognosis and said "There isn't anything else we can do for her. The surgery you performed is some of the best I've ever seen. The rest is up to her, and the powers that be."

After the Neurologist left, James decided to take a break before the next onslaught of patients started coming in. He was very tired, but that was becoming the norm lately. He took the stairs down to the cafeteria which was in the basement of the hospital. He didn't want to run into any other doctors, or nurses, right now which probably would have happened had he decided to take the elevator. He just didn't want to have to talk to anyone. He was so tired he didn't think he could make a cognitive sentence. As he reached the cafeteria, he walked over to the coffee machine, filled his cup with black coffee and sat down at a table clear across the room in the corner. He sat the coffee in the center of the table, folded his arms on the table, and leaned his head down to rest on them. He had only been there a few minutes when he heard footsteps walking across the floor, thinking, *Now what?*

"Dr. Martin," Sarah said, "I'm sorry to bother you, but a Ms. Donalson has come in to see that last emergency patient, Laurel Richards. I think someone should go up and talk to her. She seems very distressed."

"Okay," he said with tiredness in his voice. "I'll see what I can do." He hesitated a moment before he said, "I wasn't aware that she had any relatives available, or I would have talked to her already."

"I'm very sorry you weren't told, Doctor, but Ms. Donalson is not a relative, she's a friend. We still haven't been able to locate any relatives."

"Communication is the key here, Sarah. Please see to it that this doesn't happen again. I can imagine what she must be thinking about our staff, and *me* in particular," he said without letting Sarah respond. "Please call Dr. Wilson to cover the emergency room while I talk with her."

"Certainly, I'll get him right away," she said, feeling responsible for the lack of communication, and glad to leave before the reprimand got any worse. With Dr. Martin that was about as harsh as he would ever get, though. He was a doctor that all the nurses liked to work with because his demeanor was always thoughtful and considerate of others, and he had the most beautiful soft blue eyes. It was hard for the nurses to keep their thoughts together when he was around. He was gorgeous.

"Thank-you, Sarah, I'll go right up. If you have any problems in

ER, just page me, and I'll come back down." Dr. Martin got up slowly, leaning on the table for a moment while taking a deep breath, and then he headed for the elevator this time. He knew he would have to put in long hours when he started practicing medicine, but he hadn't realized the strain it would put on his physical body, let alone the day to day mental stress involved. Some days he was so exhausted he wondered what kept him going. He had been on the emergency floor for more than 18 hours, and his shift wasn't over yet. Today had been a particularly bad day for emergencies.

The rest of the doctors who had been called in for the emergency had already left the hospital. James stayed because this was his weekend to be in residence. He would sleep on a cot in the doctor's lounge, if he got to sleep at all. Sleep wasn't what he was concerned with now. He was thinking, *When really old people die, it is probably their time to go. But when young people come in, and are in such bad condition, it's hard to handle.* He had attended to several really bad cases today, even before this last case where a young woman had come in from a near fatal car accident. The other people involved in the accident had been in pretty bad shape too, but all had been conscious, and were, by now, on the mend.

This young woman, in her late twenties, had not regained consciousness, and it didn't look good. At this time in his young career, he hadn't lost a patient. He was afraid he might lose this one. And now, he had to talk to her friend, and try to console her. He wasn't quite sure what to say. He thought, *What can I tell her that won't alarm her too much, but yet prepare her for the worst?* He was not looking forward to this. It was time for his "bed-side-manner" to shine, and he felt little like shining now. Nothing ever prepares anyone for a situation like this one, but he would do his best.

As James walked out of the elevator on the third floor he headed to the nurses station to get the file for Laurel Richards. He started looking through the file as he walked down the hall to *Room 312.* He approached the room, and knocked lightly on the door.

"Hello, Ms. Donalson?" he questioned.

"Yes, I'm Kim Donalson," she said, wiping the tears from her face as she stood to greet the doctor.

"I'm Dr. James Martin. I was the administering doctor in the ER when they brought your friend in today," he said patiently, as he walked around the end of the bed and extended his hand. She reached out her hand in response to his, and they shook hands gently. He noticed the lack of strength in her grip, and realized that she appeared drained. Her emotional state was very evident, which should have been expected, but he wasn't prepared for this. He was glad Sarah had asked him to come up and speak to her.

"Maybe, you'll want to sit back down," he said gently. Kim backed up and sat down in the chair by the bed. "I'm terribly sorry that I haven't talked to you sooner. Through a lack of communication, I didn't know they had located any family or friends. Have you been told anything at all about what happened?"

"No, no, nothing, except that she had been in an accident," she said, half crying, she continued to wipe the tears from her eyes that just kept coming. Dr. Martin felt so sorry for her. This never got any easier. In fact, each time it got harder.

"Well," he started, "Your friend, Laurel, apparently was in a car accident. She was brought in here about 1:45 p.m. this afternoon. She was not conscious, and has not regained consciousness since that time. She appears to be in a coma for the time being. There seems to be a rigidity in her limbs that we can't explain at this time. We expect that to be temporary, depending on how her body reacts to the surgery we performed. Her physical body was in pretty bad condition, but we were able to fix most of that. She suffered a few broken ribs, a fractured leg, and there were some internal injuries. She had some internal bleeding from a punctured spleen. There was a large contusion to the left side of her head.

She may, at some time, need to have another operation. What concerns us most now is the damage to her brain. Her head was apparently struck by something very hard from the lower left side. We have had a Neurologist examine her, and she is now on life support. Her brain is not functioning well enough to keep her alive by itself, at this time. Respiration is controlled by the lower centers in the brain. Breathing is generally not affected by this kind of injury, but in her case, we had to attach a ventilator to help her breathe until the brain heals enough to take over. We also have her on a feeding tube." Kim gasped and put her hand over her mouth. Her mind just didn't want to accept what she was hearing.

James went on explaining her situation, "We've done all we can to stabilize her. At this point in time, the machines are doing what her body can't do for itself. We are hopeful that as soon as her body is no longer in trauma, and she begins to heal, she will no longer need the life support systems. We don't know the extent of any neurological damage that may have occurred. We can only hope that it's minimal."

He paused for a few minutes to let Kim take all this in, and then he continued, "We were not able to locate any family members before we had to make the decision to go ahead and operate. Time, sometimes means the difference between the life and death of a patient. I was told that your name and phone number were found in her purse."

"I know," Kim said, "Her parents died when she was very young. I don't know any of her relatives. She has only lived in St. Louis for a few years. She's my business partner, and...," she hesitated with the sound of weeping in her voice, "and...she's my friend." Kim dabbed at her eyes with a tissue, and tried to pull herself together. "We own a small exotic treasure shop downtown. We were supposed to meet for lunch today, and she never showed up. I was getting worried, and then I received the call from the hospital. I wasn't ready for this. I just couldn't imagine she would be hurt so badly." She stuttered slightly, "I...I...I really didn't know what to expect."

"It would help us greatly if you could help us locate a relative in the event we would need to operate again," James said.

"She was raised in an orphanage," Kim said absently. "If she has any relatives, I don't know how we would ever be able to find them. She never wanted to talk about it," she said, still wiping her eyes.

"In that case, would you be willing to take responsibility for her in case we need to make any more medical decisions?" Dr. Martin asked. "We may need to have you sign a waiver to release the hospital of any liability."

"I'm not sure I can make any decisions right now, especially any that serious. I need some time...time...to...think."

"Ms. Donalson, your friend may not have time for that if she takes a turn for the worse!" James said rather bluntly. His exhaustion was showing up in his lack of compassion for her feelings. Kim looked at him in puzzled amazement, that he had been so sharp with her. She put her hands over her face and started crying softly, as if she had lost the will to go on.

"I'm sorry," he said. "I didn't mean to upset you. I only meant that she needs your help now. There just isn't any time to debate the issue. She could take a sudden turn for the worse, and we would need immediate permission to go ahead with whatever is deemed appropriate at the time. Not that I expect anything to happen," he said, to reassure her. "We have to be ready in case there are any changes in her condition." Kim wrestled with the decision, but understood the urgency and agreed to sign the waiver. She had to do whatever possible to help Laurel even if it meant signing something that she wasn't quite sure about.

James determined that he should explain Laurel's condition to Ms. Donalson more thoroughly. He had not yet broached the prognosis of Laurel's case. Kim wanted to know more about the accident. She really didn't know exactly what had occurred in detail or, more importantly, what Laurel's future might be, if she had one. As much as Kim didn't want to think about that, she had to.

"Ms. Donalson, I would like to talk to you about what we can expect to happen in the next few days, but I think you would be more comfortable in my office. If you will, please, follow me." Kim rose from the chair, and looked over at the still, unmoving figure that lay on the bed. She leaned over Laurel and gently touched her cheek before she turned to walk away. James waited patiently by the door of the room until Kim had rounded the end of the bed. She followed him as he headed down the hall to the elevators.

"Please be seated," James said, as they entered his office. His office was the usual plush, dark paneled room that doctors have in hospitals. She sat in one of the over-stuffed chairs that were placed in front of a large mahogany desk. James followed her, walked around the desk, and seated himself in a high-backed chair that looked quite comfortable. A pen was lying on his desk. He picked it up and held it by each end as he leaned back in his chair. As he started to talk, he leaned forward, placing the pen back on the desk top. Clasping his hands together, he began the gruesome task of explaining in great detail exactly what Kim could expect.

"Ms Donalson, I'm going to lay it right on the line. The chances of recovery for your friend are not very good. Her body has been through a tremendous trauma. Even if her physical injuries were to heal, she may have brain damage."

"What are you trying to tell me, Dr. Martin? Is she going to die?"

"I'm not saying that at all. "I'm just saying it doesn't look good. She could surprise us all and make a complete recovery. These things are hard to predict. We've done all we can do. Now, it's up to her."

Kim leaned back in her chair, put her hand to her mouth, and tried to think what she should do. There were no words to say. She sat as if in a trance until James spoke again.

"The best thing you can do now, is to be there for her," he said encouragingly. "She may regain consciousness in a few days or a few weeks, it's hard to say. Right now however, all indications show that there is an unusual brain pattern, which means she will probably not regain consciousness right away. But for now, we've found that when a patient is in a coma, even for a short period of time, the best thing is for family and friends to be there to talk to them. We have noticed improvement in a patient's condition during times when loved ones are with them." He stood up and walked around to where Kim was sitting.

He sat down on the edge of the desk and reached out and took her hand. He held it for a few seconds before he said, "I know how hard this is for you. I can see it in your face. She apparently means a lot to you. It's getting late. Why don't you sit with her for a little while, and then go home and get some rest. You can't do anything more for her tonight. You can come back in the morning, and spend as much time with her as you need."

"Alright," Kim said, as she pulled her hand from his. "I'll do that. I need some time alone with her." She stood and James put his arm around her shoulders and led her to the door of his office.

"I'll be in residence tonight and I'll be checking on her all night. If there are any changes, at all, we'll notify you immediately." Kim attempted a weak smile, and headed back to Laurel's room.

Kim felt like she had been on a fast track through Hell for the past few hours. Her head was throbbing. When she reached *Room 312* she went around the bed and sat in the chair she had sat in before, and just looked at her friend lying in the bed, still motionless. Kim reached up and took Laurel's hand in hers. She held onto her friend's hand and stroked it carefully as she tried to put her thoughts in some kind of order. She had no idea what she would do next. She thought, *Maybe I should pray....*

# CHAPTER THIRTEEN

Laurel followed the hotel manager into *Room 312*. It was much as he had said it would be, Purple. The drapes, carpet, and bedspread were different shades of purple. It was really a lovely room. The manager walked over to the window and opened the drapes. The afternoon sun shone in the room making everything look warm and inviting.

"I hope you will enjoy your stay with us," he said, and then he left Laurel to herself in the room all alone. She stood in the center of the room, and turned around looking at everything in the room.

"As far as rooms go," she said to herself aloud, "this is pretty nice." It was hard for her to understand her cheerful attitude that seemed to keep improving. Her anger seemed to be lessening, much to her amazement.

Laurel decided to freshen up before going out again. She walked into the bathroom to find everything cosmetically that she would need sitting on the counter, organized very neatly. Not the usual small bottles of amenities that hotels usually furnish, but everything, including makeup. She was in awe, again, at this place. Someone had seen to it that she would not be in need of anything while she stayed here.

She wondered, *if all these things are in the bathroom, what must be in the closet?* She walked across the room to the closet and opened the door slowly. Sure enough, all kinds of clothes, new clothes hung on the rack. All of the blouses and tops were in light pastel colors, cheerful summer colors. There were various kinds of jeans and pants, a couple of dresses in floral patterns, and one shear blue silk dress. She checked the size in the neck of a sweater. It was her size, six. Shoes in several styles were lined up on the floor of the closet.

She began to think, *how did they know I would pick this particular room? I could have picked any other room or any other hotel, for that matter.* The thought had occurred to her that they had been expecting her. But, *why was she expected? Why was she the one picked? Was this whole thing planned? And, if so, by whom? Who is this "Creator" that the doctor spoke of?* "Alright," she said aloud, feeling slightly perplexed, "I guess, I am indeed, in the 'Twilight Zone'!"

Somehow, this idea didn't seem to bother her as much as she thought it should have, which surprised her. She began to find it almost amusing. The feelings of dread she had felt before seemed to be lessening too. She just shook her head, and reached into the closet for a pair of tennis shoes. She sat on the edge of the bed, and changed her shoes. Maybe she would go out right now. The sun was starting to go down, it might get cold, so she grabbed a sweater and pulled it over her head. She straightened her hair with her fingers quickly, and started toward the door. Instantly, realizing that the clerk had not given her a key to the door, she walked over to the dresser and looked around. If he left one, he had not put it where she could find it. Walking across the room, she quickly examined the door, and found that it didn't even have a lock on it. There was nothing there but a doorknob. As she stepped through the door, she slowly pulled it shut, half expecting it to lock anyway.

Laurel felt uneasy about not having a lock on the door, but there wasn't anything she could do about it now. She would ask the desk clerk about it. She walked down the hall past the elevator to the spiral staircase, but before she started down, she looked out the window to get some direction as to where she should go. She looked across several streets and saw a large green park. *This might be a nice place to start looking*, she thought. Although, she had no idea what she was looking for. *A way out perhaps…*, but that was just a momentary thought. She seemed to be enjoying herself despite what had happened. Laurel bounded down the stairs and fairly flew across the lobby floor. When she remembered about the lock she turned around swiftly, and headed for the registration desk. She had to ring for the desk clerk.

When he came in she said, "Excuse me, but there doesn't seem to be a lock on my room door."

The clerk looked at her in disbelief, "None of the rooms have

73

locks. I thought you knew. They certainly haven't prepared you very well. We don't need to lock our rooms here because no one ever steals anything or hurts anyone. Everyone respects everyone else's privacy."

"How do you know that?"

"You are perfectly safe here, I can assure you," he said adamantly.

"Well, that is a nice concept, if you really believe that," Laurel said rather dubiously. She had no time to talk to him now. She wanted to have a look at that park before dark so she patted the desk and turned to leave. She waived at him half heartedly and said, "See you later." She couldn't believe this. She had been living in a large city too long to believe anything that silly. *We'll see about that*, she thought. *I'll get a lock myself if I have to.* She wasn't about to trust that "milk toast" evaluation of honesty that he seemed so sure of. *What kind of place is this, anyway.* She had an appointment with the doctor tomorrow, and she would ask him these questions that she had been thinking about, and in the meantime, she would find out where she could get a lock.

# CHAPTER FOURTEEN

Reece Martin was in his room going over some papers. It had been a busy day at the clinic, and after the meeting in the park with his new colleagues, he was tired. He had been thinking about the patient Charles Statten had talked about. There weren't many patients, as Charles had said, that anyone spent much time thinking about since they were here such a short time. Some were only here for a few hours, some a few days, and some for a month or two. He was a little unusual himself, not quite the normal patient, if there ever is a "normal" patient. He had been here for two years, but not as a Spanner. He had made the decision to stay almost immediately. Then, his status changed from a Spanner to a Stayer.

He continued to think about Charles' patient. *Why would this one be any different than the rest,* he thought? Charles seemed to think her worth spending a little time with, and Reece was glad that he would be included in her next visit with him. Reece was relatively new to this world, if you can call two years new. There was still a lot he didn't know about this place, but he was learning fast. He felt that he might be able to make this person's stay a little easier to understand, since he had already been through what she was going through right now. It had been hard for him at first too, but he was adjusting very well here. Actually, he liked it here. He had work he enjoyed, friends to spend time with, and such a feeling of well being was with him at all times.

There had never been any question in his mind about whether or not he would stay, or that he had made the wrong decision. It had been like a rebirth for him, and he intended to stay forever. He had no family that he acknowledged on the other side. As far as he was concerned there was no one to miss him, or for him to miss. He had family secrets that were best left behind, and he didn't want to remember, or deal with them ever again. He had more friends here than he had *ever had* in his own world. He intended to stay forever, and have life eternal. He had found the place of his dreams. He belonged here.

Reece looked forward to this meeting tomorrow with Charles' patient. He thought he would go to bed early tonight so he would be rested for the meeting. Although, before he got ready for bed he walked over to look out the window. He had a nice view of the park It was a lovely place. That was where he had met with his friends earlier, and where he had found out about this interesting patient that Charles was talking about. He could see a few people walking around outside. It was such a lovely evening, he changed his mind about going to bed early. He thought, *I think I'll take a walk instead.* He actually, wasn't as tired as he had originally thought. Some fresh air might make him sleep better, anyway. While looking out the window, he thought he saw something going on over by the park. He was curious to find out what was happening over there. He had taken off his shoes so he slipped them back on and headed over to the park.

Laurel had reached the park and was about to enter it when something hit her like a brick wall, and knocked her to the ground. She had walked into something. She didn't know what had happened, and she thought she must have slipped on something. Looking around, seeing nothing made her feel kind of stupid, falling down like that. She got up and started walking toward the entrance again. She hit it again, but this time she caught herself before she fell. A third, time she was much more careful, as she approached it more slowly. She reached out her hands, feeling her way, when she actually touched something. There was nothing there for her to see. She felt her way along this thing, whatever it was, that appeared not to be there. She couldn't get through it, she couldn't see it, but it was there.

"What in the world is this?" she asked herself. She started edging her way around the park with her hands up in the air sliding them along as she walked. In the background she started hearing noises. A crowd was gathering. They were smiling and laughing quietly and pointing at her. She did look a little ridiculous with her hands up in the air apparently touching nothing. She stopped, turned around sheepishly, smiled and said, "Hi!" to the crowd. They giggled and left. She felt ridiculous.

After the crowd left, she turned around and was about to try again, when someone said, "You can't get in that way." She turned with a jerk to find a handsome man with blond hair standing there with a smile on his face.

She hesitated for a moment, smiling back at him, and then she asked, "Then how do you get in?"

"Well, actually, it's off limits to you," he said rather shyly, as nicely as he could. He didn't want to offend her.

"Oh?" she questioned rather indignantly, "and why is that?"

"The only people allowed into this particular park are Guardians and Stayers. The Spanners are only allowed in this park if they decide to become Stayers. And, it is obvious that you are a Spanner, since you can't get in," he said confidently.

"I don't understand," Laurel said with a confused look on her face. Besides being puzzled by not being able to get into the park, she was wondering who this stranger was, possibly in his early thirties. Tall, blond, and handsome, with the bluest eyes she had ever seen. She mixed that up a little, but it fit. *You don't have to be dark to be tall and handsome,* she thought.

"It's not that hard to understand once you know why it's off limits," Reece said. "The Guardians need privacy sometimes, and this park provides that."

"Privacy from what?" Laurel asked suspiciously. "Why all the secrecy around here? I just start feeling like it's not so bad here and then, something like this happens and I wonder what's going on." Laurel sat down on the curb, put her hands over her face, and just shook her head in disbelief.

"Who are you?"

"My name is Reece Martin. I live in an apartment around the corner from here, and he pointed in the direction of his apartment. It was next to the building that Laurel was staying in.

"What a coincidence," Laurel said. "I'm staying in that building right next to yours. I guess we're neighbors."

"Hmm…so we are. Would you like to go and get a cup of coffee,

Neighbor?" he offered. It was already dark by the time Laurel had reached the park earlier. She had noticed a man standing a few yards away who seemed to be looking her way. He just stood there watching as she tried to get into the park. At first, she thought this was the same man, but as she looked that way again, she noticed that the other man was still there. The area around the park was well lighted, even so, Laurel wasn't sure she wanted to be out on the streets alone so she accepted his offer.

"Yes, I think I would. I need something to calm my nerves. Maybe you can help me to understand what's going on around here, if you don't mind?"

"I'll try," he said quietly. He didn't want anyone to hear him. He wasn't quite sure why he felt he should be quiet. It just seemed to be the right thing to do at the time. Sometimes, there was an underlying feeling that something, or someone was watching him. Whether it be good, or bad, it was a little unnerving. He had noticed the man down the street too, but he hadn't said anything. He didn't want to upset this pretty, young woman. He mostly just wanted someone to talk to. He realized that he hadn't even asked what her name was.

"By-the-way, what's your name?" he asked as they walked along the street.

"My name is Laurel Richards, and I don't really know why I'm here, or how long I'll be here, and I'm very anxious to go back home. I feel like I'm lost in a dream, and I can't wake up. Or someone won't let me wake up."

Reece just smiled at her remark, and they walked until they reached an outside cafe. Reece motioned to the waiter, holding up two fingers indicating that he should bring two drinks over to their table. The waiter nodded, and went to get the drinks.

After a few minutes Reece said, "I can understand your feelings of confusion, because, I've been there."

"You've been where?" Laurel asked surprised. Reece pulled out a chair for Laurel to sit down. "What do you mean by that?"

"Please sit down. He continued, "I'm not sure you're ready to hear this."

"And, exactly when will I be ready?" she asked. "I can't seem to get past everyone's idea that I'm not strong enough to hear what's actually going on here. I see no point in waiting any longer to find out everything I need to know. The longer I wait, the more confused I get," she pleaded.

"I told you I'm a 'Stayer', didn't I?"

"No, you didn't. You said that only Guardians and Stayers could get into the park. I assumed that you were a Guardian. The doctor told me a little bit about that. He said he was a Guardian, but it was all so confusing, I'm not sure I really grasped what he was saying."

"Well, this may be a long evening. I'll tell you everything I can. At least, everything I know," he said.

"First, can you tell me why there appears to be so much secrecy?" she asked. "I haven't been able to find out much of anything."

Reece looked at Laurel with compassion for her helplessness in this situation. He knew exactly what she was going through, although, he didn't know where to start telling her what was going on. Especially since he wasn't sure how much she already knew. He didn't know how much of the truth she could handle right now.

"How long have you been here?" he asked her.

"As far as I can figure out, about a day and a half. Although, I'm not sure how long I was on the road before I got to Nora's cafe," she said. "And, the next thing I knew, I was in Dr. Statten's office lying on a cold metal table draped with a white sheet."

"Dr. Charles Statten?" he questioned. "You're Charles' patient?"

"Yes, I guess I am. He's the only doctor I've seen since I've been here. I suppose you *could* say I'm his patient. Do you know him?"

"Yes, indeed I do. I'm supposed to meet with him tomorrow to help him with a patient, and I believe that you may be that patient. We thought, Dr. Statten and I thought, that perhaps, it would help you if someone, like me, who has been through what you are going through right now, were there to talk to you. I thought it might give you a better understanding of everything."

"Somehow, I'm beginning to feel like a lab experiment."

"Oh! No, please don't feel that way. That wasn't our intention at all. It was my suggestion to him that I talk to you. It wasn't his idea."

"Well, are you going to tell me what's going on, or am I going to have to wait until tomorrow?"

"How about if I tell you about myself tonight. I…I mean about my being a…'Stayer', not my personal self," he stuttered. The waiter brought their order. Laurel sipped her drink, noticing that it was one of those wonderful waters that they had offered her earlier. She thought that if she listened to what Reece had to say about himself, maybe, just maybe, she would start to get some idea about what this place was all about. It was worth a try so she agreed to listen to what he had to say.

Reece explained that being a Stayer was the best of all worlds. He could live eternally, could have anything he wanted, at any time he wanted it. He also said that he had been given an opportunity to go back, but had refused to go. That it was his choice to do so.

"Everything here is about choices," he said. "If my physical body should die in our world, I can leave this place and go on to Heaven, if I wish to. At this time, I have no desire to leave this place, to go back or to go beyond. I think it's wonderful here! Have you noticed the smells, the tastes, and the vivid colors that we encounter each day?" he said with great gestures of his hands and arms. He had gotten up, and was walking around the table smiling. Other people in the cafe were starting to watch him. When he noticed this, he sat back down and talked more quietly.

"Everything here is so intense, it's exhilarating. It makes me feel alive! Everyday, I wake up happy, and can't wait to begin my day. I say to myself, 'what GOD has created here is beyond belief'."

"You said 'God'. Dr. Statten referred to someone as, 'The Creator,' and someplace called, 'Elysian Fields.' Are we talking about the same person, and the same place?"

"Yes, you have to remember, I'm from our world, not theirs. He's still God in Heaven to me."

"I'm sorry, but I am having a hard time understanding why you stayed here, and gave up everything you had when you could have gone home where you're friends and family are."

"I don't have a family, well, anyone that I care about," he said, telling what he thought was a small lie. My family doesn't give a damn about me. There's no one back there that I feel a need to acknowledge, I'm free. I've made new friends here. Friends who appreciate me, for myself, and my abilities. I feel like I'm part of this place now."

Laurel was amazed at the happiness that Reece exuded. *Was this real?* she asked herself. She could not imagine that she would ever want to stay here, as nice as it was, she still wanted to go home. She was raised in an orphanage, and had no family either, they had that in common, but apparently nothing else. She loved her life in her own world, and she intended to get back there somehow. She didn't know how, but she would find a way. This she vowed to herself.

It was getting very late, and Laurel was getting tired. Actually, she felt near exhaustion. Maybe all this was just too much to comprehend.

"I think I would like to go back to my apartment, if you don't mind. Will you be there with me at Dr. Statten's office tomorrow?" she asked. "I would appreciate it if you would be there. I know that I don't really know you, but I do feel comfortable with you." She hadn't wanted to admit it to herself, but she felt very comfortable with him. If nothing else, he seemed honest. He was someone from home. Someone she could feel an attachment to, at least for the moment. In this world where everything seemed outside of her realm, he was someone to hold onto.

"Of course, I'll be there. I'll walk you back to your apartment." The strange man that they had seen earlier was still lingering along the street. Laurel sensed that he shouldn't be there. So, she mentioned it to Reece. She was glad that Reece had offered to walk her back to her apartment. Not having a lock on her door was going to be a worry after seeing that man. Reece assured her there was nothing to worry about, although he wasn't sure he was right himself. He just knew what he had been told. There wasn't supposed to be any crime here. To his knowledge, there hadn't been any since he had been here. He had a sense of foreboding about the man too, although he didn't reveal his feelings to Laurel. He didn't want her to have something else to worry about. *She has enough on her mind to keep her busy for quite awhile,* he thought.

Reece didn't know that Laurel was already worried about this man, who seemed vaguely familiar to her. She tried to put it out of her mind with little success. She knew she didn't want to be out alone on this night.

Reece left Laurel at her apartment, and walked on to his own apartment. He started thinking about the man on the street. *What could his motive be for skulking around,* he thought. *There would be no point in his trying to hurt someone. No one can be harmed here. There is no advantage. So, why is this man acting so strangely?* He decided he would ask his colleagues about this one. He couldn't get over his uneasiness about this stranger. He could certainly understand Laurel's anxiety. Maybe, there were still things he didn't understand about this world that he should know about. It was the first time he had felt like this since he had gotten here. He usually felt very comfortable living here even though his physical body was still living on the other side, and he had no intentions of leaving or going back. Even if his physical body died, he had no intentions of going beyond this place. His reasons for staying were not exactly as he had portrayed them to Laurel. He hadn't felt it necessary to tell her the real reasons. The reasons he had told her were valid, but not entirely true. He was happy here, and he didn't want to dwell on any other reasons now. It was his choice to stay, and it was none of anyone else's business. So, he left it at that.

After being left at her apartment door, Laurel walked up the spiral staircase and down the hall to her room. After she entered, closing the door tightly behind her, she just stood there looking around at the room for a few minutes before she walked across to the window. She thought she would see if Reece was still within sight. He was gone, but in the shadows she could see a dark figure. Goosebumps went up and down her spine, as she backed away from the window. She stood by the side of the window partially hidden by the curtain, and peeked out again. The man just stood there, lurking in the shadow of the trees. She couldn't imagine why he was there. He had apparently followed them. *For what reason?* she wondered. She backed away from the window, slowly, making sure he didn't see her. She started to shake nervously. She sat on the edge of the bed trying to calm herself.

Laurel tried to reason with herself as she thought, *He can't hurt me, no one can be hurt here. They've told me that several times. He's probably not even looking at me,* she thought. *I might as well relax. He's down there, I'm up here, out of harms way.* Even with that idea in her head she slowly, but deliberately walked over to a chair, picked it up and placed it in front of her door propping it under the doorknob. *At least, if someone tries to get in I'll hear the chair move,* she thought. She decided that if she went to sleep she might be able to put these thoughts out of her mind. She found a night gown in the closet, changed into it, and went to bed. Hoping for better things tomorrow.

Laurel sat up in bed for a few minutes thinking about the meeting with Dr. Statten, and she was beginning to feel a little anxiety. She was hoping he could give her enough information to logically deal with everything that had happened during the last 36 hours. *Only 36 hours! It seems like it's been an eternity,* she thought as she slumped over on the pillow and fell into a fitful sleep.

# CHAPTER FIFTEEN

Ed bent down to tie his shoe. He had been out walking for the evening when he thought he saw the young woman who had just left Nora's place. He had been in the cafe reading the newspaper and drinking coffee when he decided he needed to get out for awhile. Go someplace…any place…he needed some fresh air. After awhile he passed by the "Un-accessible" park that had always intrigued him. For some unknown reason he had never gained access to the park, even though he had become a Stayer. He saw this young woman, who he was sure was the same one who had arrived here a just few days ago, trying to get into the park. He stood by the light post and watched her.

He thought, *I'll just watch to see what happens with this person.* But then, another man whom Ed had never seen before walked up and started talking to her.

Ed had nothing else to do so he thought he would hang around and see what they were doing. He thought it would do no harm if he followed them.

"I'm just curious," he said. But, he kept his distance so they wouldn't know what he was doing. No point in getting too close. He didn't want anyone asking him what he was doing. He saw them go into the sidewalk cafe. They were there quite awhile and he had almost decided to leave, but then, they got up and started walking somewhere. He kept a short distance behind, keeping them barely in sight.

*This is fun,* he thought. Kind of brought back memories of doing this before, but he couldn't remember when. It just seemed familiar. When the two people he had following reached the hotel, they both entered the building, and soon, the man she was with left the building and walked on down the street. Ed thought he would stay a little longer in the trees along the side of the street. The evening was nice, as were most nights, so he lingered. He didn't really know why he was doing this. He just felt like he had done this before. It made him feel alive. He hadn't felt this way in a long time, and he didn't want the feeling to end.

He watched the man until he entered the next building. Then he wondered, *What would be wrong with going inside the hotel where the girl had gone?*

"Couldn't hurt anything," he said aloud. So, he crossed the street and entered the building. There was no one in the lobby when he walked in. He stood perfectly still for several minutes, glancing around the room like a frightened deer. His adrenalin was starting to flow. He walked quietly across to the stairs, not knowing where he was going or why. Although, he thought he saw someone looking out the window on the third floor. *Maybe it was that girl.* Without anymore deliberation he decided to go up to the floor where he was sure the girl might be.

Carefully, he started up the spiral staircase. There was a wicked smile on his face. He had always wondered what happened to all the people who came through the cafe. Maybe, this was a chance to see for himself. This girl left as suddenly as she had come, as so many others had done, and Ed wanted to know why. But, that wasn't his main reason for being here tonight. It was only an excuse. The real reason wasn't even clear to Ed.

When he reached the top of the spiral staircase on the third floor he hesitated only a moment before starting down the hallway. He walked up and down looking at both sides of the walls.

"This is weird," he said quietly. "There aren't any doors, just walls. I thought there would be rooms up here! This can't be right, there have to be rooms here somewhere." For a moment he tried to convince himself that this was okay. He just didn't know where the rooms were. Then, reality started to set in. He was trapped! This frightened Ed, more than he had ever been. *What's going on?* he thought. "I'm gonna' get outa' here!" he said, as his eyes widened with fear. He turned to go and immediately saw that the staircase was gone. It disappeared so totally that it seemed never to have existed. He stood looking around himself unsure of what to do next. He appeared to be in a long box with no windows, no doors, no stairway.

Breaking out into a cold sweat, he couldn't believe what was happening. At first, he didn't want anyone to know he was there. He tried to control himself because he wasn't supposed to be in this building.

*I should never have left the cafe*, Ed thought. *I should have stayed where I was safe.* Then, fear clutched his heart like a vice, and he started to panic. He felt his chest tightening. He placed one hand on his chest as he ran down the hallway, looking for a way out, breathing heavily, pounding on the walls, screaming. He was frantic now, and he didn't care who knew he was here. He wanted someone, anyone, to help him. He felt like he was in a coffin. He was having trouble breathing. With disbelief in his eyes, he realized that he was actually suffocating! He could feel his own footsteps pounding in his ears. The sound was deafening. He grasped the sides of his head with his hands as he continued to run down the hall. As he reached the end of the long passage way, there was a flash of light, and, Ed was gone...

Somewhere, far away from *The Keeping Place* in the real world in a hospital for the criminally insane, there was an empty bed. Ed had passed into another dimension. One where he wouldn't be able to hurt anyone ever again.

# CHAPTER SIXTEEN

Laurel awoke suddenly. The sun was coming up and light was filtering through the room. Considering the fears she was entertaining last night, she was surprised that she had slept so well. The chair was still in front of the door where she had put it to try and protect herself from the strange man who had been lingering around the hotel last night, and also from anyone else who might be about. She got up and walked across the room and looked cautiously out of the window to the trees below, just to see if the stranger might still be standing there. The man she had seen the night before was gone. Feeling relieved she showered and dressed quickly. She wanted to look around town again for awhile before her 4 o'clock appointment with Dr. Statten. She wanted to be able to ask some intelligent questions about this place. Like, where were all the children, dogs, and cats. She hadn't seen any since she had gotten here.

As she glanced around the room in the daylight she caught a glimpse of herself in the mirror above the dresser, ran her fingers through her hair, and said, "I think I'll get a hair cut while I'm out too." She wondered if they cut hair the same way here as they did at home. It would be a curious experience. She needed a lift, and getting her hair done had always had that effect on her.

After she had dressed and was feeling hungry, Laurel headed down to the lobby. Like usual, there was no one around. She decided to walk over to the sidewalk cafe and have breakfast. As she reached the cafe she could see several couples sitting around tables, almost the same as she had seen before, except they were different people. Again, they all appeared to be engaged in happy conversation. She thought she would sit close enough to one of the couples to hear some of their conversation. As she sat down, the waiter walked over to take her order.

"Good morning, Miss, would you like to see a menu?" he asked cheerily.

"Good morning to you too," she said smiling. "Yes, I would

please." Laurel had no idea what kinds of food would be available here. The water thing had been an unusual experience. She wasn't sure what to expect. While she had been talking to the waiter, she noticed that the couple she sat next to had left the cafe. *Well, so much for that thought.* She wasn't close enough to hear any of the other customer's conversations.

*I guess I'll have to get information from some other source,* she decided.

The food on the menu was basically the same as it was anywhere so she didn't spend any more time thinking about that. She ate a simple breakfast of an English muffin and fresh fruit. Then feeling refreshed, she headed out on her adventure for the day. She still had several hours to kill before her meeting with the doctor. She wouldn't try to get into the park again. That was a chilling experience that she wouldn't soon forget. At least, for now she would stay away from that place. Maybe, sometime later she would try to get in by some other means, if she were still here. What those means might be wasn't something she wanted to deal with right now, but the thought remained in her head. *I'll get in there somehow,* she vowed to herself. Why this was important to her wasn't clearly evident. There was just something about the park that drew her to it, and it intrigued her. She felt that at sometime in the near future she would be able to get in there, one way or another.

Laurel walked along the street looking at the small shops on both sides. It was a quaint little town. No cars, just people milling around, going in and out of the shops. She tried to stop a lady who was about to pass her, but the lady just smiled at her, and kept going, as if she were in a trance. She tried again, the same thing happened. She tried several times, same results.

"I'm not sure these people are real." she said out loud. She had once read a book where the women had been made into robots, and she noticed the similarities, although these people didn't speak. She decided to be silly and she jumped in front of the next person who passed, no response. The person just dodged around her, still smiling. She kept doing that, acting ridiculous, and the men and women just kept going wherever they were going! After a few minutes, she stopped, feeling completely stupid. She had always been a shy kind of person, and this was way out of character for her. She had no idea how to interact with these people. At this point, it didn't seem like it was possible. They apparently didn't want any involvement with her. Either they wouldn't or they couldn't respond to her. She felt alienated and lost again. A feeling that was never far from her mind.

She decided to step inside one of the shops. As she entered the shop the clerk asked, "May I help you?" Laurel had a shocked look on her face. Here was a real person. Someone who she might be able to communicate with.

"Why...? Why don't these people on the street speak?" Laurel asked without greeting the woman properly. She hadn't felt the need for the niceties that usually accompany greeting a person for the first time. She just wanted to get some answers.

"I don't know what you're talking about," the clerk said with an astonished look. Trying to change the conversation quickly, she moved out from behind a counter, and asked, "May I help you find some dresses?" The woman looked up and down Laurel's frame, noticing her attire. Laurel was dressed in a red tank top, faded jeans, and tennis shoes. These were the clothes that had been provided for her in the apartment. This was a dress shop, and apparently that was all that was in it. Laurel could see she wasn't going to get anywhere with this woman.

Shaking her hand in the air with an attitude of "what's the use," Laurel said, "Never mind," and she turned and walked out the door. She wasn't interested in clothes right now. Besides, there were plenty of clothes in the closet in her room. She had more important issues that needed to be handled. It was obvious that she wasn't going to find out anything from anyone around here. She decided to go for a walk down the street to see where it led. She wouldn't stop until the street stopped. So, off she went with determination, paying no attention to anyone else on the street, as if it made any difference, since they wouldn't respond to her anyway. She would walk until it was time for her appointment with Dr. Statten. Perhaps, she could find out something on her own. At least, she would give it a try.

Laurel wandered around all day, and saw more of the same buildings, the same shops, everything the same...same...same.... The only differences were the colors of the buildings. She had been to Bermuda once, and these houses reminded her of the colorful houses there. It was a pretty town, almost too pretty. She felt tired, exhausted actually. It was almost time for her appointment. She turned around and started back to that part of town, hoping that this time she would get some real information that would help her to know what was happening in this place.

Just when she was about to leave the town area to go to her appointment with Charles she found a beauty shop. She walked in and said, "Do you take walk-ins?"

The lady at the counter said, "Yes we do. Come right on in. We have an opening right now."

*How convenient*, Laurel thought. She showed Laurel to a chair, wrapped the plastic coverlet over her and started fingering her hair.

"How would you like it cut Miss," she asked.

"I think I would like it quite short." Laurel tried to talk to the lady, but she only responded with yes and no answers. She couldn't get any real conversation going so she gave up asking any more questions, and just closed her eyes and enjoyed the experience. When the haircut was finished Laurel looked in the mirror and was pleased with the results. She didn't have to pay for it, and that made it even better. *What a place*, she thought. *Hard to get used to, but nice.* Then, she thought, *What am I thinking? Why would I think anything here was nice?* She shook her head and tried to shake some sense into herself. She decided she shouldn't let that happen again. She would have to be more careful.

Since this was a small town it didn't take Laurel long to reach the doctor's office. As she reached Dr. Statten's office she was told to sit in the waiting room because Dr. Statten was meeting with a colleague.

"He'll be with you in a few minutes," the nurse assured her.

Laurel took a seat and waited. She hoped he wouldn't keep her waiting very long, as she was anxious to meet with him again. She had lots of questions to ask.

Reece had worried all night about that stranger hanging around Laurel's apartment. He knew he shouldn't have, but he couldn't help himself. He decided to go early to his meeting with Charles, and ask him about this man. Charles was working in his lab when Reece arrived. An assistant took him to where Charles was working. He looked up surprised at seeing Reece so early. He hadn't expected to meet with him before they talked to Laurel.

Charles still had feelings of distrust for this man. Stayers were not people he usually had any dealings with. He wasn't quite sure how to take Reece. He seemed nice enough, but Charles was feeling imposed upon. Laurel was his patient, and he normally didn't have any interference from anyone.

Trying not to show his jealousies, he greeted Reece, "Well hello, Good to see you again," he said not really meaning it, but trying to sound sincere. Without waiting for a response, smiling, he reached out for Reece's hand, and grasped it firmly.

Reece responded with the appropriate greeting, and said, "I hope you don't mind that I came a little early. I have a few questions I would like to ask you. You seem to know more about this place than most of the others, and I would like to pick your brain, so to speak." That remark eased the tension right away. Charles felt more at ease. At least, this man understood that Charles was a capable physician. Asking for his advice put a new slant on things. He thought, *Maybe I should try to keep an open mind about this guy after all.*

"Alright, what is it that you have questions about? I might be able to shed some light on the subject. At least I'll try," he said with a smile, indicating that he probably didn't know everything, but would give it a shot.

"Let's go into my office where we'll be more comfortable. It gets a little noisy out here," he said, lowering his voice, "It's also more private." Reece was glad for the privacy. He didn't know how much of what he was going to say was supposed to be heard by anyone else.

Reece followed Charles to his office, and stood waiting for an invitation to sit down.

"Please, sit down," Charles offered. "What is this 'thing' you need to talk to me about? Does it have anything to do with our meeting today?"

"Well yes, in a way it does. I...quite by accident...met your patient, Laurel, last night."

Charles looked stunned, as he said, "Go on."

"I saw her trying to get into the park," Reece said. "She seemed very distressed. I approached her, not knowing that she was your patient until some time later. But, the problem is not with her. It's actually about a fellow that we saw lingering around. I think he was following us. What I don't understand is, why? Why would he be lurking in the shadows, and follow us. As far as I can see, there would be no purpose for him to be doing that, if you get my drift? Is there any way that he could hurt her, or am I missing something here? It was my understanding that no one could be hurt here in any way. This incident reminded me of living in my world, where if someone were following us, like this man did, we would be very concerned with our safety, and would probably have called the police. But, since there are no police here I really didn't know quite what to do."

Charles started to relax a little, and he smiled at Reece, as he said, "I get your point, but I can assure you that you were in no danger. If there is someone who threatens anyone, either physically or otherwise, he will be taken care of. It is absolutely an impossibility to hurt anyone here. That's one of the great things about living here. You could say we are invincible. So...I don't entirely understand your concern. That kind of problem doesn't usually occur, but if it does it's usually taken care of immediately. Do you know who the person was?"

"No, I only know that Laurel was very upset about it. We didn't talk about it much. I didn't want to alarm her any more than she was already."

"Did you tell her anything about this place?" Charles asked.

"I only told her about myself, being a Stayer, that was all."

"Well, then, I'll tell her everything she wants to know about the way things are here. And, about that stranger...I'm sure he has already been taken care of."

# CHAPTER SEVENTEEN

Nora got up early. She realized that Ed had not come home last night. That was odd. He was always here. Most of the time she had a hard time getting him out of bed early enough to do the morning chores. He was a late sleeper whenever he had the chance. She, to her own amazement, because she was usually a very light sleeper, had slept very well and was surprised that she had not awakened in his absence. She busied herself getting ready to open the cafe. She thought, *He'll probably be here soon. He surely wouldn't make me do all this work by myself this morning.* Ed wasn't much of a man, but at least he was good help.

Nora started the coffee, made the juice, and then looked out the window. There were two people coming down the highway. She could see them in the distance. Thinking this would be a busy day, she wondered, *How am I going to handle everything without Ed.* At 6 o'clock a.m. she went ahead and opened the cafe just in time for the newcomers to arrive. She was actually open 24 hours a day if anyone came and needed help, but she only officially opened each day at six for her regular customers, *I can't keep the customers waiting because of my problems,* she thought. She had a few regulars who would come in early for coffee, and of course, each day she never knew when strangers would be here. She needed Ed to help with the regulars while she dealt with the newcomers.

By, noon Nora was getting concerned. Ed still hadn't come home. When he left the evening before, he said warily, "I'll be back in a little while." She had not been concerned, except that it was rare for him to leave the cafe. He usually just sat around drinking his coffee and reading the newspaper after the chores were done. A walk would probably have done him good. Maybe it would help him to be less sullen. Some days he was hard to take. Except for the extra work she had to do, she was feeling relief that she didn't have to deal with him this morning.

Nora was told she was never to leave the cafe unattended. She wasn't sure what she was supposed to do. Or if she were supposed to do anything at all. She fretted about this for a couple of hours while serving customers, and taking care of the two newcomers. Then, as if from nowhere, a man walked through the door. Nora hadn't seen him coming, she had been too busy to pay a lot of attention to what was going on outside the cafe. He was a nice looking man, about her age, and smiling as he approached her.

"I've been sent over to help you." he said very politely. "My name is Phil, Phil Peterson."

Nora smiled back at him, and said, "Please sit down. I'll get you some coffee. We have quite a few things to talk over, and I'll fill you in on what your duties will be." This man had come as mysteriously as Ed had. Guessing that, *this must mean Ed wasn't coming back*, she questioned what had become of him, momentarily. Then, she assumed that possibly the same thing had happened to him as happens to everyone else, like the people who were here before her, who left suddenly.

Nora had felt like she was in a rut, and nothing would ever change for her. This turn of events might prove to remedy that situation. Since she was married to Ed, she wondered if she would miss him. She looked down at her left hand with a slight smile, her wedding ring was gone.

# CHAPTER EIGHTEEN

Laurel was getting tired of waiting, and was just about to check with someone to see if they had forgotten her when an attendant came to take her to Dr. Statten's office. As she walked in, she saw Reece sitting in one of the chairs. She was glad he had come. They said the customary greetings, and Charles said, "Please sit down Ms. Richards."

"We've been waiting for you."

"Thank-you, please call me Laurel," she said timidly, as she sat in the overstuffed chair next to Reece.

"Alright, now that everyone is comfortable, where would you like me to start Laurel?" Charles said.

"How about at the beginning. I may have missed a few details the last time we met," Laurel said without a bit of hesitation.

"Alright, that sounds like a good idea. It won't hurt to go over a few things again." He paused for a moment and then said, "First, from the beginning, you are still aware that the only reason you are here is because you are in a coma, right?"

"Yes, I know that is what you are telling me. Whether or not I believe it is another thing. I'm not convinced you are telling me the truth mainly because of all the secrecy. If everything is on the up and up, why aren't you telling me everything?"

"You have only been here a short time, and you weren't ready to hear everything as soon as you got here," Reece added.

Laurel looked at Reece as Charles said, "That's exactly right. Thank you for adding that Reece." Charles looked directly into Laurel's eyes and he continued, "We try to help you understand as much as you can, as soon as you are ready for the information. If we flood your head with too much, too soon, you might not be able to handle it. And, as you said, you may have missed a few things that I told you before. It's better for you to ease into the reality of the situation. I can see already that you are more receptive today than you were on our first meeting." Laurel continued to listen more intently.

"You were brought here for safe keeping, which is why this region of the universe is called *The Keeping Place*. This is a long story, and I hope you will let me tell you everything without interruption. If, after I tell you all of this, and you have any questions, I will answer them then. And, Reece, if you would like to add anything I would appreciate it if you would also wait until I have finished. I don't want to leave anything out so I am asking you this favor also." They both agreed and he began the story that Laurel had been so very anxious to hear. Reece was also interested in hearing the story again.

Charles started by telling them, "In the Book of Remembrances, The Creator has said that 'Many worlds have I created'. Most people think that he meant physical worlds. That is not necessarily the case. He also meant spiritual worlds, as well. In this world, which is like a spiritual world, you are physical in every sense of the word. Your life is practically the same, except that you cannot be physically harmed. In that sense, you are spiritual. Your body is the same as it is in your world. You can touch, feel, smell, etc. just as you could in your own world. Although, those senses are much more acute here, as I am sure you have already experienced." They both nodded, but didn't interrupt.

He continued, "Your body has to heal for you to be able to go back to your world. A coma is a way the body protects itself from unbearable pain and suffering. There are times when the mind would not be able to withstand the pain. The brain transports the patient into a coma. Thus, you are placed here. After your physical body has healed sufficiently you will be given a choice to go back, and you will be instructed as to what you will need to do to make that happen. But, until that time you are required to stay here and follow our rules. That is the only restriction you will encounter while you're here.

You can stay here as long as you want after your body and mind have healed, but it is not recommended. Although, that *is* one of your choices. Everything in life is about choices, as I have said before. Choices that you make determine what your life will be. You have a life in your world, and if you are meant to live there, you should go back. If, for some reason you prefer to stay here, just as Reece has chosen to stay, that is entirely up to you. We would welcome you into our community should you make that decision. There are some things that you cannot experience here without becoming a Stayer. For instance, like the park that you tried to enter. That is off limits to Spanners."

"How did you know that I tried to enter the park?" Laurel asked. "Do you have hidden cameras out there too?"

"Absolutely not," Charles said disgustedly. "As you can see, Reece was here before you came in, and he mentioned it to me. Now, May I go on without any further interruption?" She nodded sullenly realizing that he was right, and she should have guessed that Reece would have told him how she had stupidly tried to enter the park.

"Should you decide to stay, that park and many other things will open up to you. That, and numerous other things that I can't explain to you at the present time. Although, you would have to make the decision to stay before everything could be revealed to you. If we told you all of those things now, it might influence your reasoning and cloud your ability to make the right decision for your well being. Your decision has to come from the heart, without any interference from outside influences.

As, I said before, you must be ready with your decision when the time comes because you will only be offered one opportunity to go back. When *The Veil* beckons you must be ready to go. Once you have made a decision to stay, it will be final. You will not have another opportunity to go back. That's why I emphasize how important it is to make that decision as soon as possible, and to be sure that it's the right decision for you. Now, if you have any questions I'll try to answer them."

Laurel thought it sounded a little frightening to think that there was only one opportunity to leave. She was sure she would be ready. The trip through *The Veil* sounded like when you take a bus or a plane, or any kind of public transportation, you're always afraid you'll miss it, even when you have planned everything perfectly. The very thought of having to stay here for the rest of her life scared her to death. There was something unnatural about this place, and she didn't feel comfortable here. Perhaps, that would change with time, but she didn't think so. She hoped she wouldn't have to find out.

"About this '*Veil*' you mentioned," Laurel asked, "how does it differ from a portal?"

"The difference between a portal and a veil is that, a portal only opens at specific times," Charles said. '*The Veil*' I speak of stays open all the time. At any time you could be pulled back through. Thus, the importance of being ready to go when the time comes. And also, a portal isn't always at the same place, whereas *The Veil* is in one place only in this world."

"Okay," Laurel added, "And where, exactly is that?"

"You'll know soon enough."

"There it is again, the secrecy."

"It's not secrecy," Charles insisted. "It's just that you cannot know where it is until you are ready to leave here. If you wandered into it before you are ready, before your body and mind are healed, it could be devastating. Possibly life threatening. We are protecting you, simply doing our jobs."

"Alright then, if you insist on not telling me," Laurel said, thinking she would find out where *The Veil* was by herself, "another question that has been bothering me is why don't the people on the street respond to me when I talk to them?"

"They don't see you, unless they are meant to see you, unless it has something to do with their recovery, and you *don't* see most of them." he said. "There are many more people out there that you will *never* see unless you become a Stayer. There are things they are concerned with other than you. Since you, and they, probably won't be staying, it's not important for them to interact with you because they have other objectives on their minds. You needn't be concerned with them either. You may be here only a short time, and it clutters your mind and theirs, with unnecessary thoughts. Most of them are healing too. It is imperative that we alleviate any and all stress to your brain for it to heal properly. You are allowed to see and interact with those people who are important to you during your stay with us. This is all done for your well being, believe me," he said.

Laurel took all this in while contemplating her next question. She was glad to hear the part about her *probably not staying*, because she knew she would be ready to go, if and when the opportunity arose. In her mind, there was no decision to be made. She had already made it!

"How will I know when it's time to go back?" she asked with concern."

"If you don't mind, Charles," Reece said. "I can answer that."

"Go ahead," Charles said with relief. He didn't know the real answer to that question. He had a clinical answer, but thought since he hadn't actually been there it was good that Reece wanted to handle that question. Having been born here, and having never experienced that particular situation, it was hard for him to respond so he let Reece continue.

"It wasn't a hard decision for me to stay," Reece started. "I've felt at home here ever since I came. I've been accepted by everyone, and I love it here. But, putting that aside, when the time comes, you will feel a strong pull on your mind and body. Mostly, in your mind. An almost uncontrollable urge to go somewhere. You may hear voices several days before *The Veil* beckons. Voices that are trying to call you back through. You may also experience headaches, but not everyone does. You will have time to get to where you need to be in time for the opening. I had a hard time resisting, but I knew I absolutely did not want to go back. I was afraid that I wouldn't be strong enough to resist the pull, but your heart knows where you really want to be. If you are worried that you might accidentally miss your time of departure, don't. If you really want to go, nothing can stop you. It's actually harder to stay than to leave." That relieved Laurel's mind, a little. She smiled appreciatively at Reece because he was concerned enough to help her understand, but again, she couldn't imagine why anyone would want to stay here. Why they would resist going back home, as Reece had done was hard to understand.

Laurel thought there must be more to this than she could conceive. Especially, since she couldn't find out everything unless she became a Stayer. It looked like to her, that you would need to know all the information they were withholding to make a reasonable decision.

"Perhaps, there are wonderful reasons to stay here, but I can't see that they would be better than the reasons to go home," she said.

"We want you to make your decision without any outside influences, as I said before," Charles said to Laurel. "If we paint this lovely picture of what our world really is (he gestured with his hands), you might make the wrong decision for you, personally. And, we don't want that. That's why you are not given all the information about our world. You should only stay if that is what is right for you. Most people are much better off going back where they came from." He hoped she would make that decision, to go back, but he wasn't allowed to influence her either way.

"It seems that we are making an argument more for staying than for leaving, but that is not what I am trying to do. What we are really trying to do is to guide you into making the right decision for you. Whether that decision will be to leave, or to stay is irrelevant. Whatever is right for you is what's important," Charles said.

Laurel thought about what he had said for a few seconds and then said, "I think I understand that now, but I have another question. "I want to know how they, or you, knew exactly what I would need while I am here. The room is exactly what I would have wanted. The clothes in the closet fit me perfectly. Even my makeup is exactly what I would have bought for myself. Even at Nora's place everything was perfect. How did you know I would be here? It's almost as if someone knew I was coming. Were you expecting me?"

"Yes, we did know, as soon as you were transported here," Charles said. "The Creator knows everything. He prepared us for your coming. We have workers here whose only job is to make your stay as comfortable as possible."

"Why haven't I seen any of them?" Laurel asked.

"Well, you actually have seen a few of them. Nora is one of them. The desk clerk at your hotel is another. In fact, Reece and I are also here to help you. As I said before, you will only see the people that are pertinent to your well being while you are here. Many others will go unseen until it is necessary for you to see them."

Laurel was getting tired, feeling overwhelmed again with what she had heard. She was actually feeling exhausted again, possibly from all there was to comprehend, but she had one more question. She leaned forward, rubbed her brow while shaking her head, as if she needed to remember something, and said, "You said before, the other day, that I would need to know more information about this place in order to live comfortably while I'm here. Exactly, what did you mean?"

He looked at her with raised eyebrows, and then at Reece before he said, "There are certain things, behavioral attitudes, that you are required to live by while you are here. It is simple enough. You are expected to respect everyone with whom you might have an encounter. I have a handbook that you can read that might clear up a few things for you. It is just general information."

Charles was remembering how she had reacted on her first visit with him, and thought she could probably benefit from reading the book. In his opinion, she had been very disrespectful to him and his staff, but considering the situation he would try to overlook her behavior.

Laurel took the book and thought, *How ridiculous! You're thrust into a place like this, and they give you a handbook?* She thought it was ludicrous. Almost laughable! She was too tired to argue with him today so she thanked him for his time, set up a time for another meeting leaving the two men alone in Charles' office. Still, she had many unanswered questions, and she would be glad to talk with them again. She would go back to her hotel room and rest for awhile. She couldn't believe the overwhelming tiredness she felt.

Laurel had no idea what her physical body was going through on the other side which, had she known, would have accounted for the unexplained exhaustion she felt periodically. Here, she felt totally physical, as if nothing at all were wrong with her body except for the extreme tiredness that would almost overwhelm her. She was trying to understand what he meant when he said this was a spiritual world in a physical sense. *How could that be possible*, she thought? She only knew she needed to get some rest or before long, she would not be able to respond to anything or anyone coherently.

Reece stayed to talk to Charles for a few minutes after Laurel left. "I think I'll talk to her again on my own, if you don't mind Charles?"

"Fine with me. What you do on your own time is up to you. If you can help her with this transition that would be great. We're here to help our patients all we can. She seems to be relating to you in a positive way. I can see she is having trouble comprehending all this. I do think you should be careful, though. She's a hard case. There appears to be some hostility in her. Have you noticed it?"

"Yes, I have, but I can understand why she acts that way. She just wants to go home, to get her life back. I think she may have been a very vital person in our world. A person who loved life more than most. I think a lot of people get so bogged down with everyday problems that they forget what real living is all about, me included."

"Perhaps, you're right Reece. Do what you can. I will see her again tomorrow. If she reads the booklet I gave her maybe that will clear things up a little more, and I can answer any other questions she might have. If we work together on this maybe we can help her get through this." They shook hands and Reece left the office.

He thought, *I think I'll try to catch up with Laurel. I really would like to talk to her again, by myself.*

Reece felt like Laurel was still floundering, and he wanted to help her as much as he could. And, besides that, he enjoyed her company much to his own surprise. Since he had been here, he had not found anyone he thought was as intriguing as Laurel. Not just medically, but as a person. There was just something about this girl. He wasn't sure why he felt this way, but it was worth the time he was willing to spend to get to know her better. That is, if she would allow it. He realized that any kind of long term relationship wasn't possible, because she could leave at any moment, but he wasn't thinking about that now. The only thing he was interested in at this time was possibly some companionship, although, he had not actually admitted that to himself. His association with his colleagues, both men and women, was very fulfilling, and he enjoyed it very much. Female companionship was very lacking in his life, and perhaps, that was what was drawing him to Laurel. He would have to hurry to catch up to her now. He headed out the door and could just see her in the distance.

"Laurel," Reece called out. "Wait up!" He had to run to catch up with her. Laurel turned hearing her name.

She looked at him with a surprised, but pleasant look on her face and said, "Reece, What are you doing here? I thought you were staying to talk to Dr. Statten."

"I did, for a few minutes, but then I wanted to talk to you again. I hope you don't mind. And, hey, you cut your hair. I like it!"

"Thank you, and of course I don't mind. What do you want to talk to me about?" she asked, as she tossed the handbook in a garbage can as she passed by.

"Everything, anything!" he said with an excited sound in his voice. "I want to tell you anything you want to know about this place. About life in general, about happiness, about all this," he said with his arms up in the air and spinning around like a school boy. Laurel couldn't help but laugh at his animated attitude. He seemed so happy that it was contagious. For the moment she almost forgot her circumstances. The tiredness she had felt before seemed to be disappearing. She noticed the change as soon as she stepped outside of the building. She was almost happy for the first time since she had been here.

*This person is really fun to be with*, she thought. They walked along, laughing and talking like young people in the real world. Reece told her about all the wonderful things he had experienced since he had come to *The Keeping Place*. Hard as it was to imagine, she was intrigued with this place that was so beautiful, and with these people who appeared to be so kind. Much different from the impressions she had when she first arrived. It had only been two days since she had been placed here, but it seemed like an eternity. So much had happened in so little time, but she was beginning to feel, comfortable.

# CHAPTER NINETEEN

FOUR MONTHS LATER:

Kim kept working at the store trying to put everything out of her mind except the work at hand. She was busy putting out the new items that had just arrived. She always enjoyed this part of the work. It almost seemed like Christmas to open the boxes and see the new trinkets. She found it to be very interesting work. Kim had had no choice but to go to Greece without Laurel. Although, it was not in the same time frame they had originally planned. She had waited until Laurel was stabilized, and out of immediate danger. Life goes on in the retail business. It doesn't stop because someone is unable to do his or her job. Her father had taken over the shop for her while she was gone, and he used some of the staff from his own store to fill in when he was unable to be there. The trip had done Kim a world of good, just to get away.

The evenings, after long days with vendors, had been a time when she could relax, and completely forget the real problems she had left at home. The beaches there were so peaceful, she almost wished she could stay there forever. However, her sense of responsibility was so overwhelmingly traditional, that staying was of course, out of the question. This was the first shipment from that buying trip. Laurel was still in the hospital in a comatose condition. She had not, as they had anticipated, come out of the coma.

Kim visited Laurel as much as possible, but the business had to be run. She had to keep it going the best she could. Her father would stop by once in awhile to help her out. He had stopped by this afternoon to relieve Kim so she could visit Laurel at the hospital. This was becoming her daily routine. Open the store, work for awhile, and then have someone fill in while she went to the hospital. She felt she needed to be there as often as she could for Laurel's sake. She was running out of friends and family to help her out. She wasn't sure how much longer she would be able to depend on them. She felt like Laurel was her responsibility, not theirs. Even though, her friends and family had been wonderful, she didn't want to burden them any more than absolutely necessary. They had been there for her, just as she was there for Laurel. Though, the strain was becoming unbearable.

Dr. Martin had told her she should consider taking Laurel off life support. He said that Laurel's physical body was healing better than he had expected, and they, he and the hospital staff, would like to remove her from the life support machines to see if she could function without them. He wasn't sure what her mental capacity would be if she were to awaken from the coma. Her brain waves appeared to be normal, but it would be hard to predict. Especially, considering the condition she had been in when they brought her into the ER. Dr. Martin thought it a miracle that she had lived, and yet, she was recovering physically in record time from the injuries she had sustained. The staff and he were puzzled at why she hadn't come out of the coma. It appeared to be a very deep coma. Sometimes, when a patient is taken off life support, it shocks the body into waking up. It was suggested to Ms. Donalson that she consider that procedure. Even though Laurel's body was healing, Kim had a hard time handling the situation.

Seeing her friend lying there, comatose, was devastating. Kim would be there when they changed her bed, rolling her to keep her from getting bedsores. She would even help with the daily physical therapy. Laurel's hair had grown in where they shaved it off for the operation, and Kim cut her remaining hair to match that which had grown back in. She would comb her hair and talk to her without ever getting even the slightest response. Despite the condition Laurel was in, there would only be a few small scars around her hairline. Looking at her porcelain skin made Kim feel as if she were looking at a beautiful mannequin, lifelike, yet never moving. Like Dr. Martin or, James, as he had asked her to call him, had said, "It was a miracle that she had lived."

Today, when Kim came in, they had just finished bathing Laurel. Kim walked over to her bedside, leaned over and brushed the hair away from Laurel's forehead with her hand. She looked down into her friend's face and thought how peaceful she looked. Quite a change from when they first brought her here. Kim almost envied that peacefulness. The trauma that Laurel had experienced on that day, and the mental anguish that Kim had endured since the accident, was consuming Kim's life. She had no life! Just an existence. As she stood there, apparently lost in thought, James walked into the room. She saw him from the corner of her eye, and she looked up with no smile, no emotion. She was beyond feeling. Her emotions had been on a roller coaster for so long that she was almost in a "shutdown" mode.

Although the accident had physically impaired Laurel, emotionally it had shaken Kim to her very soul. At times, she wished that she had been the one there, lying in the bed. She wasn't making light of the tragedy that had befallen Laurel, but right now she wasn't sure who was in worse shape.

James walked closer to the bed, still looking directly at Kim, he asked, "Ms. Donalson, How are you today?"

"I don't know. I just don't know, and I'm sure you really don't care what I'm feeling today."

"Quite the contrary, I care very much about how you feel." It hadn't been just an empty remark he said to reassure her. Being a compassionate person who really did take an interest in his patients, he felt as if he had been slapped in the face with her remark. He really did care about her feelings. He had seen her at least once a day for the past four months, and had grown to like her very much. He considered her to be a friend. Of course, it was just a patient/doctor relationship. He had more interest in Laurel than in Kim at this time, and since she was Laurel's friend, he felt close to her too.

Earlier on this day, James had been in the room with Laurel, checking her charts, wondering why she hadn't awakened from the coma. Medically, as far as he could see, there was nothing that should keep her in the coma. Her body had mostly healed. He was anxious to remove the life support system to see if she could sustain life without it. The head injuries, as bad as they were appeared to have healed or, so they thought. But, something still wasn't right or she wouldn't be lying in this bed unable to respond to anyone or anything. Perhaps, they had missed some crucial element in her healing process. He had stood beside the bed and looked into Laurel's face, thinking what a pretty girl she was, and what a shame it was that she had been thrust into this world of pain and sorrow. Now, he had come to see her while Kim was here to pose the question of removing the support system.

He started, "Ms Donalson...."

Kim interrupted him. "Please don't call me that. I've asked you to call me Kim. After all this time together, I don't think we need to be that formal," she said with an air of exasperation."

"Alright Kim, Have you had time to think over the idea of taking Laurel off life support?"

"Yes, I have thought about it, very seriously, as a matter-of-fact, and I'm not ready to do that yet. I would like to give it a little more time." James was shocked. He was so sure she would agree to it that he hadn't even thought what he would say if she decided not to do it.

James was speechless for several seconds before he said, "You *are* aware that taking her off the machines could actually bring her out of the coma, aren't you?"

"Yes, but what if her body rejects the process, and it puts her in more danger. Couldn't she go into shock and die?"

"There is always that possibility, but since her injuries have healed so well, we haven't even considered such a consequence. More than likely, if it doesn't bring her out of the coma, her condition will remain stable and she will go on much the same as she has for the past few months, only she'll be doing it on her own. It would be much healthier for her. There would be less deterioration to her body if she can maintain her bodily functions by herself. I thought we had explained this to you thoroughly enough for you to understand this."

"I know you did," Kim said with tears welling up in her eyes, "But I can't do this right now. I need some more time. This is a terrible responsibility. It's like putting Laurel's life in my hands." It made Kim feel like she was playing God.

"I'm just not ready to make that kind of decision. At least not today. Just give me a few more days, and I promise I'll try to make the right decision for her." She hadn't mentioned it to anyone, but one of the reasons she felt melancholy was that today was Laurel's birthday. How could she make a life and death decision on Laurel's birthday. She decided to mention it to James so he could understand her reluctance, but then she thought, *Why would he care, Laurel was just another patient. He probably has dozens more just like her.* She stood there in silence hoping he would go away and leave her alone. James stared at Kim in disbelief. He couldn't believe she could be so weak. A decision that might save Laurel's life, keep her from becoming a vegetable.

*How much more time does she need? Four months is a long time to be held in suspended animation,* he thought. In James' mind, dying would be better than this. He turned toward the door to leave, but before he left he said, "Your friend's life is being held in the balance. You can go on feeling sorry for yourself or you can make a decision that could possibly bring her back. What would you want her to do if you were the one lying on that bed?" He left the room with a manner approaching disgust, and Kim was left alone in the room with Laurel.

James had no idea how cruel those words had been to her. They had cut through her like a knife. She sat down by the side of the bed, and after several minutes of soul searching, realized that he was probably right. He had been blunt, but maybe she *had* been thinking more about herself than she had about Laurel. She was feeling sorry for herself, wondering, *Why me?,* when she should have been thinking about the condition Laurel was in. It had been tremendously difficult for Kim, to take on such a responsibility. She could have walked away, and said it wasn't her responsibility, but who would have taken care of Laurel then? She would probably have become a ward of the state. That would have put her back exactly where she had started, just like in the orphanage.

At that moment, Kim decided that in a few days she would tell them to go ahead and remove the life support system, but she just couldn't do it today. She took Laurel's hand in hers, squeezed it lightly, tried to smile amidst the tears and said, "Happy Birthday, Laurel."

# CHAPTER TWENTY

Laurel was sitting on the edge of her bed, thinking what she should do today. She was incredibly bored. She hadn't found anything to occupy her time since she had been here, other than talking to Reece that she enjoyed doing. She hadn't tried to find a job because she hadn't thought she would be here this long. Besides, she wasn't sure people who were visiting had that option. That idea had not been mentioned to her, along with a lot of other things that hadn't been mentioned. Like, *what was she supposed to do with her life while she was here? Maybe, she should have read the handbook.*

It had been four months since her arrival. She found that she wasn't as tired as she had been, at first. She felt like there was nothing at all wrong with her. And, why should she feel like anything was wrong since she was still not aware of having had any kind of mishap, even though they told her she had been in a car accident. It was still hard for her to believe.

Laurel decided that she would try to find Nora's cafe today. It had been quite awhile since she had arrived here. She thought she should try to find out exactly where she had come into this world. No one seemed willing, or able to help her find her way home. Apparently, no one had tried to call her back, and she wondered why. Surely Kim would have tried. She was the only friend Laurel could have relied on.

Since no one seemed to care enough to bring her back, she would have to try to get home from this side of *The Veil* by herself. She decided that if she were able to find that road by the cafe, maybe she could find a way out of here. That road was the way in…maybe…it was the way out. At least, it was worth a try. Maybe Reece would help her. He knew how much she wanted to leave this place. She had many talks with him about his wanting to stay, which she could never quite understand. To her, this place was like living in limbo. Nothing stimulating enough to call living, as far as she was concerned.

Laurel thought it funny that she had never tried to find Nora's cafe before. The thought just kind of came to her, almost like in a dream. Laurel hadn't seen Nora since she had arrived. Another thing she found odd, there didn't appear to be any phones in any of the buildings. But, there had been one in Nora's place. She remembered trying to make a call before they took her away from there. Although, she hadn't actually *used* the phone. Maybe it hadn't been a working phone at all. Since that time, she couldn't remember having seen a phone anywhere. Everyone walked whenever they went anywhere.

The area they called town was small enough that you could walk to everything. She had almost gotten used to that. Her feelings of anger had passed. Most of the time she felt quite happy, along with most of the people she saw on the streets that appeared to be in some kind of subliminal bliss. That did seem odd to her, but not enough to upset her. There was something that made a person feel comfortable here. She wasn't sure what it was, or why it was, but it kept people happy all the time. People just didn't get angry. That in itself was starting to annoy her. She began to think that perhaps there was something in the food or in that extraordinary water that they served everywhere that might be responsible for keeping people happy.

That being in her mind, Laurel thought she would try to abstain from the water to see if there was something to this idea of hers. It was just a vague idea that faded in and out of her mind. There seemed to be something trying to block her thinking processes, but it was indefinite. She couldn't quite put her finger on it. Whatever it was, she could think quite clearly each morning, but by evening she had all but forgotten the very ideas that had been bothering her. Every morning it was like she had new thoughts…like, starting all over again. She was never able to get any further with those thoughts. She decided she would mention this to Reece, but not right away. She was going to experiment with it first.

When Laurel reached the bottom of the stairs and walked into the lobby, she saw the desk clerk talking to one of the maids, whom she had never seen, clean the rooms. The rooms were always clean when she returned. No matter how long she was gone. She thought that if she went back up stairs right now, the room would probably be clean, already. She thought, *I think I'll run back upstairs right now and see if I can catch the room unmade.* She turned suddenly and dashed up the stairs. As she left the staircase and ran down the hall, she almost slid past her door. Catching herself she leaned back and opened the door quickly. Sure enough, everything was clean as a whistle. She couldn't help laughing at herself for being so silly, but the bed was made, the curtains pulled back, everything picked up and put away. *Amazing,* she thought, and she wondered, *how do they do this?* She stood quietly by the door and then instantly she remembered that she had almost forgotten what she was planning to do today. No more distractions. She would continue toward her goal which was to find Nora's cafe.

This time, when Laurel reached the lobby, she hurried on outside to the street. She was feeling hungry. She would stop somewhere and eat breakfast, but she would not have any water. She walked along the street admiring the beauty of this apparent spring day, until she came to the first cafe. It didn't matter where she stopped to eat because all the cafes had the same kinds of food, but yet she never tired of it. They all had outdoor tables. She had not seen a drop of rain since she had gotten here, but everything was still green and beautiful, not dry at all. She sat down at the first table she came to. Immediately, a waiter came to take her order.

When she declined the water the waiter said, "Are you sure you wouldn't like some water?"

"I'm absolutely sure. I'll do quite nicely without water, thank you. I would like a glass of milk instead please." When the waiter brought her order about ten minutes later, he brought a glass of water anyway, along with the milk. She thought, *I must be right about the water because they seem to want me to drink it whether I want it, or not.* "Well, they won't get the satisfaction," she said to herself, quietly. She quickly ate her breakfast of a bagel, fruit and milk, and as she stood to leave, she looked around to see if anyone was watching. Then seeing that no one was paying any attention to her, she gently tipped the table, and the glass of water fell and spilled all over the table. The empty milk glass also fell and rolled to the floor.

The crashing sound brought the waiter immediately. Laurel acted as if it had been an accident, exclaiming how sorry she was.

While cleaning up the mess the waiter said, "I'll bring you some more water right away."

Laurel said quickly, "No, No, It's okay, I'm leaving anyway." And she hurried away.

# CHAPTER TWENTY-ONE

Charles was sitting at his desk going over some papers when he ran across a copy of the report he had submitted to his Superiors on Laurel Richards. He sat looking at the report wondering how she was doing. He knew it had been a particularly difficult time for her. Even more so for her than to most, because she had been more determined to analyze every thing that was happening to her. She questioned everything. He read over the report again, thinking that perhaps he should have told her other things that were involved with her time spent here. Other things that might make her stay more comfortable. He had told her most everything, but there were a few things that he hadn't felt necessary to burden her with. Like her state of mind while she would be here. She probably needed counseling, but she wouldn't submit to it. He had told her he could arrange counseling, but she hadn't seemed interested. *Maybe, I should have insisted*, he thought. He was going to contact her and suggest it again, as soon as he had time. Provided she had time before being called back through *The Veil*.

There was never much warning as to when a Spanner would be offered the choice to return home. He decided that he should leave work this morning and look for her. He left his office early and headed into town along the tree lined street enjoying the brisk morning air. He reached the sidewalk cafe in a few minutes, and in the distance he glimpsed a person he thought might be Laurel so he hurried on.

In Laurel's hurry to leave the restaurant, she almost ran into Charles. He was right, it had been her sitting at the cafe, and he intended to join her, but she had suddenly jumped up to leave. He thought he had seen her tip the table as he approached the cafe, and he wondered what this was all about.

"Hey, Hey! Where are you going in such a hurry?" he said, laughing. He had to grab her to keep her from smacking right into him. He held her arm gently and smiled as he waited for a response.

She was shocked to see him, and embarrassed. As innocent as it was, she felt like she had been caught with her hand in the cookie jar.

Laurel was relieved that it was Dr. Statten and not some stranger, but she wasn't going to let him know that as she said, "Let go of my arm!"

"Oh! I'm sorry," he said apologetically, I didn't mean to frighten you."

"You didn't! I'm terribly sorry that I almost knocked you down, but I have some place to go, and I guess I was in too much of a hurry."

"And, where might that be, if I'm allowed to ask?"

"Well, since you asked, I guess I can tell you," she said. She had some questions she wanted to ask him anyway. She thought she would take advantage of this chance meeting. At least, she *thought* it was by chance. "I have some questions I would like to ask you."

"Sure, we can sit here or just take a walk, and talk."

"I don't think I want to stay here after what I just did," she said, anxious to leave the cafe.

"Actually, what did happen here?"

"I don't want to get into that right now, I'll tell you later," she said, thinking that if she could help it, it would never come up again. She didn't know how much she could trust him. *He was one of "Them,"* she thought. They walked on down the street away from the cafe and after a few silent minutes he asked her how she was doing.

"I'm doing okay, I guess, if you can call existing okay." Charles wasn't exactly surprised at her attitude.

"Well, maybe, I can answer some of the questions that have been bothering you. You've missed a few meetings with me lately." He picked up her hand and patted it. She wasn't sure if his demeanor was sincere or condescending, as she pulled her hand away. *He is very attractive*, she thought. Although, he had the mannerisms of a man much older than he appeared to be.

She hadn't thought about it until now, but everyone here was very attractive. Even the few people that she would see walking down the street or in the cafes. That was another thing that seemed very odd to her. She decided to ask him about this since he was asking for her questions.

"Why are the people here so pretty? And why aren't there any children? Or cats and dogs? And why isn't there any rain?" These questions took him by surprise. He thought she might have more serious things to ask him, but he just laughed and started to answer her questions one by one. But first he asked her to call him Charles instead of "Dr. Statten."

"It seems a little too formal for the occasion," he said. Laurel thought so too, although she wasn't sure she should become that familiar with her doctor. Especially, one she knew so little about. But, if that was what he wanted, it was little enough to concede to find out what she needed to know.

He began, "There are children here, but they are kept in a separate place. They are so delicate that we don't want them to interact with anyone except the nannies. When they are away from their parents it is so much more traumatic for them, than, say for yourself, as an adult." She couldn't imagine it being any more traumatic for anyone else, than this had been for herself. It was a rather selfish thought, but she didn't know it at the time, having never had children of her own.

"You can go visit the children sometime if you would like. We do have to monitor those visits though…kind of keep them to a minimum," he added.

"I would like that," she said sincerely.

He went on, "Dogs and cats go somewhere else. They have a special place for animals of all kinds, and as far as there being no rain here, you're right about that. The reason for that is because the water comes from the ground. Instead of rain coming down, the water comes up. It's as simple as that. And about the people here being pretty, he smiled and said, beauty is in the eye of the beholder. Now, any more questions?" They came to a grassy spot along the street and Charles led Laurel to a place to sit down on the grass. She finally smiled back at him. She had enjoyed being with him for this while, and he had opened a door of understanding between them. He was a lot nicer than she had expected him to be. Her questioning was not over.

She started again, "I still have some unanswered questions. Like, where is the cafe where I came into this world? Where is the highway that I was walking down? Is there some reason I'm not supposed to know that?"

"Of course not," he said. "Well, partially. You can know where the cafe is, but you can't be taken back where you came into this world."

"Why?" she asked bluntly.

"There's that question again, 'why?' Because it would do you no good. You're forgetting, I told you things only happen here for your own good, and that would serve you no purpose."

"Are they afraid I'll be able to go back by my own volition?"

"No, no, nothing like that. That would be quite impossible anyway. You can only go back when you are called back or at a time that is right for you. I know, before, I said you might harm yourself if you wandered into *The Veil* by accident, but in reality, to protect you from peril, *we* prevent you from going there until the healing process is complete. It may seem deceptive to you, but that's just the way it must be for your safety."

"Deceptive is right. I have felt deceived in so many ways here, and you keep saying that I'll be called back. If that *is* true, why haven't I been called back? It's been four months," she said with tears coming into her eyes.

"I can honestly say, I don't know. That is not anything we can know here. We are just as surprised as you will be when you get the opportunity to leave. One day it will just happen. You will know when the time comes, but you won't have much time. However, there will be enough time to make your decision. As I said before, just be ready."

"I was on my way to Nora's cafe when I ran into you. I wasn't quite sure how to get there, can you take me there?" she asked him while drying her eyes.

"Of course I can, why not."

"I have one more question."

"Go ahead, I can't wait for the next one," he said, laughing slightly, and then they both laughed. Most of her questions had been very light hearted, but she still had some serious questions swarming around in her head. She decided to go ahead and ask the question that was bothering her most right now. "Is there something in the water here that makes people happy?"

"You're joking, right?"

"No, I'm not joking. There must be something here that makes everyone so happy. It's not natural. I have felt an overwhelming feeling of well being. I thought maybe it was, in the water," she said hesitantly. He rolled back on the grass and laughed so hard that he was almost embarrassed. Laurel was feeling insulted.

"You may think these questions are very trivial, but to me they are very real and important."

Then, he sat up, apologized for laughing, and became more serious, as he said, "Believe me, there is nothing in the water! That feeling of well being is because of the healing process that is going on in your head. The better you feel, the more you are getting back to normal. You seem to forget that you have been through a tremendous shock. Your physical body was almost irreparably damaged."

Laurel feeling less offended said, "I guess, since I have no memory of that happening to me, I can't imagine that anything has changed with me, except being in this place where I've been put. I'm still having a hard time realizing that anything, at all, happened to me."

"I can relate to that, but, I can assure you it did happen, or you wouldn't be here." Charles stood up, reached down offering his hand to Laurel, pulling her up while saying, "We had better get going before it gets too late."

After she was standing, Laurel deciding to make light of the situation, asked teasingly, waving her arms around in the air. "And, where are the bugs, flies, mosquitoes, ants?"

Charles answered with a smile on his face, "The sins of your world are not ours. Bugs do not exist here in my world, and from what I've been led to believe, it's a wondrous thing. We don't have to suffer for your transgressions."

Laurel took his arm and said, "I don't think they were all mine." They both laughed and started walking toward their destination.

# CHAPTER TWENTY-TWO

Laurel and Charles had walked for quite some time when in the distance they could see Nora's cafe. Memories flashed back to that fateful day when Laurel had first come to *The Keeping Place*, as they called it. She didn't like those feelings, and was almost sorry she had asked Dr. Statten, or Charles, as he preferred to be called, to bring her here.

Nora was busy washing off the counter in the cafe when she saw two people come through the door. Laurel smiled in Nora's direction as she entered. Nora dropped her wash cloth, and her mouth fell open in amazement. She had never had anyone, ever, come back to see her. She had helped hundreds of people come through *The Veil*, but never had anyone returned. She had always wondered what happened to them, if they went back or stayed. She recognized Laurel right away as being one of "hers," because it hadn't been very long ago, only four months, since she had been here. She wasn't sure what her name was, but she immediately recognized Laurel's face. She remembered her because she was different than most of the others, in a good way.

"Why, girl, what are you doin' here?" Nora said with a chuckle in her voice. She was glad to see that Laurel was alright. She had always worried about her Spanners. Especially, this girl. Nora walked around the counter to greet Laurel and gave her a big hug. Laurel returned the gesture. It almost felt like home to her. That was an odd sensation, and it surprised her, but she felt closer to home here where she had come into this world than she could have ever imagined. Tears filled Laurel's eyes…an emotion she hadn't expected.

Charles wasn't quite sure how to handle what happened next. Laurel and Nora sat down, and started talking about everything that had happened since Laurel had left the cafe on that day four months ago. Quickly at first, but then they both relaxed and enjoyed a pleasant conversation. Nora had no idea what happened to the Spanners when they left her place, and Laurel had never really grasped what Nora's role was here in connection with her, and others, or even if there were others. Nora had made the decision to become a Stayer probably before she was completely ready, even though her heart knew what her decision was to be. Now, she realized why she was needed here, she was compelled to be here. Laurel only knew that Nora had helped her when she felt the world had fallen down around her. Nora and this place had been an oasis in a desert full of doubt and fear. Laurel remembered how kind Nora had been to her when she had come from out of nowhere into this place. She would always value her friendship for that.

Charles thought that it might be too much for both of them to gain this much knowledge in one afternoon. He suggested that he and Laurel leave before they wore out their welcome. Nora didn't want them to leave so soon so she offered to get them something to drink.

"Alright," Charles said. "But, only for a little while longer. We don't want to be out too late. I'd like to get you back to your hotel before dark." Laurel had a puzzled look on her face, wondering why they needed to be back before dark. Nora served drinks to her visitors, taking one for herself, as well. She mentioned to Laurel that Ed was no longer with her. Of course, Laurel couldn't remember much about Ed because she had no actual contact with him. She just remembered a quietly strange man sitting there watching her, making her nervous. There was something that lingered in her mind about him, but she wasn't quite sure why. She didn't waste time trying to figure it out. She just put it aside for better, more important thoughts. Like trying to find a way to get home.

After spending a pleasant time visiting with Nora, like they were old friends, Laurel and Charles said their goodbyes to Nora, and left for the walk home before the sun went down. Laurel thought that this reunion had been kind of strange. She had never known Nora before the day she had come to this world, but yet, this afternoon it had seemed like she had known her all her life. They talked like they had some kind of bond. Maybe, because they had experienced this connection when Laurel had entered, they felt a need to help each other.

This meeting had helped Nora to realize that she had a purpose.

That she was really doing some good, and she needed that feeling to continue. She had felt her life was pointless, but now she could see what she was doing was worthwhile. After they left, Nora went back to work with a renewed sense of importance. She would welcome the next guest with open arms. Not that she hadn't in the past, but now she understood why. Laurel had the same pleasant feeling too, and she intended to come back to see Nora soon, but without Charles. She wanted to talk to Nora alone. Maybe Nora knew more than she was letting on about everything here, and if she did, Laurel was going to find out what it was. Every bit of knowledge she could gain would help her with her endeavor to leave this place. Now, with each passing day, her contempt for being here was growing. She wanted to go home, and she would do everything possible to make it happen.

She really enjoyed the day with Charles in spite of everything that had happened previously. Considering the mistrust she had felt toward him in the past, she was pleasantly surprised. Also, she couldn't seem to shake this feeling of happiness that she had experienced all day, and then it suddenly entered her mind. Like a voice speaking inside her head, she realized that today had been her birthday.

The evening stars were starting to come out by the time Charles dropped Laurel off at her apartment. Charles thought the visit with Nora quite boring, but he could see it had done a world of good for Laurel. Anything that would help Laurel to cope was welcomed by Charles. He really liked her, although, he was trying to keep his desires under control. *Desire is a strange choice of words,* he thought. He had no intentions one way or the other toward this girl. He knew she could leave at any time. He would be careful not to enjoy the friendship too much. This was an unusual involvement for him. *She is just another patient,* he kept telling himself. He had never spent this much time with any of his other patients. *She was different...more interesting,* he thought.

Charles had been sure to get Laurel back to her apartment before dark. There was an unwritten law that Guardians were not to be out late at night with Spanners. It was more for their good than anything else. It had never been a problem for him before now. He had never been placed in a situation like this, until today. Even though, he thought it wouldn't be too serious a thing to be out in the dark with a Spanner, he didn't want to have to deal with any problems now. He lived by the rules, and he had always been happy to oblige his Superiors.

There were no organized religions in *The Keeping Place*. Religion was a pagan idea that seemed to have a hold on other worlds, and which had no place here. The thought of having to be taught morality was unheard of. The "good" ruled everything, and should "bad" influences come into this world, they were dealt with swiftly and thoroughly before anyone had any doubt that good would, indeed prevail. Charles had no trouble following the rules.

After leaving Laurel, Charles decided to see if his friends were in the park. Several of his colleagues were there sitting at the picnic table as usual. Frank, his best friend, was there again with several others.

"Hey bud, how are you?" Frank asked in his usual jovial manner.

"Well, I've just spent a lovely afternoon with that patient I told you about a few months ago."

"She's still here?" Frank asked. "It's been nearly four months, hasn't it?"

"Yes, it has," Charles said. "She has been here longer than most, I have to admit."

"You're putting in some extended hours, aren't you?"

"I think it's time well spent, Frank." Charles said more seriously. "I think it will help her to heal faster if she knows a little more about everything here."

"Well, if you're sure. You don't want to get involved with a Spanner," Frank said with a wink.

"Oh, there's nothing to worry about. She is just a nice young woman who is really confused. I feel an obligation to her. It's solely a doctor/patient relationship. Have you ever thought what it must be like to be placed in a situation like the Spanners are placed in? I imagine it must be quite frightening. What do you think?"

Frank looked at Charles with a wary expression on his face, as he said, "You had better be careful, Dr. Statten. (He would call him that when he was trying to be "officially" facetious) You may be getting in over your head, and into things better left alone. It's not our responsibility to worry about these people any more than just taking care of their physical needs. If I were you, I wouldn't be talking too loudly. Anyway, I haven't given it much thought. They are usually only here a short while, and I have better ways to spend my time than speculating about their precarious situations. And, maybe you should do the same." Suddenly, it became very quiet. Frank had never spoken so sharply to Charles before. He was shocked, and he hadn't appreciated the warning. He had never been reprimanded for his so called "bedside manner" before, and he didn't like it. He stood to go. The others, Mary, Bill, and Ryan hadn't spoken up in his defense. Charles thought they seemed as shocked as he had been.

Frank said, "Come on, sit down. Let's talk about something more exciting than our patients. I've been thinking about doing that golf tournament next weekend. How about you guys all coming too." Everyone started talking excitedly. They all thought the tournament was a grand idea. Frank was pleased that his attempt to change the subject appeared to be working, but Charles remained standing, ready to leave. Frank realized that he might have overstepped his bounds with Charles. Anyway, it was none of his business what Charles did with his free time. If Charles wanted to get involved with a Spanner, why should he care? But, he did care. He knew what happened to those who didn't follow the rules, they just disappeared without a word, and Frank didn't want Charles getting into something that he might regret. Charles was his friend, and he thought he should warn him about associations that might be harmful to him. He was only trying to be helpful. This friendship they had was important to him, but he wished he hadn't spoken so sharply in front of their other friends. It was too late now, the damage was done. He would make amends somehow, but Charles wasn't willing to let him do that right now.

Mary stood, gave Charles a little hug, and said in a flirty way,

"Can't you stay for a little while longer?"

"No, I have to go. I'll talk to you later...about the tournament." Charles wasn't thinking about golf as he hurriedly walked away. He was surprised and distressed at his friends' lack of compassion for their patients. Maybe the Spanners *were* only here for a short time, but it was up to him and his colleagues, as doctors, to make their stay as pleasant as possible. That was a switch from his own previous attitude, but no one mentioned that. And, as far as any involvement with a patient, he kept telling himself he was just doing his duty. The job he was trained to do. *And*, he thought, *I'm doing a damn fine job of it at that.* He was angry at Frank for even suggesting that he would get involved with a patient. The very thought of it was ridiculous. Just a few minutes ago, he had been in such a good mood, and now all that had changed. He, to his own surprise, had begun to think more like Reece. He walked back to his hotel feeling more depressed and alone than he had felt since his parents had left him so many years before.

Charles' friends, whom he had expected to support him, had disappointed him. Maybe he should think about doing the tournament. He had been working too hard. Lately, all he could think of was Laurel. He needed to get his mind off his work for awhile. Even so, he couldn't help but wonder why Frank got so upset about his remark about the Spanner situation. *Could there be more to it than he knew? Was there some underlying reason for Frank's concern?* The more he thought about it, the more he became preoccupied with the thought that there might be something he didn't know about the Spanners, something that might do harm to either himself or others. He was concerned enough to find out. He would talk to his Superiors about this. *And yet, if there were something he didn't know, and if he were doing something he shouldn't be doing, maybe he wouldn't want anyone to know. But, that was crazy. He had always followed the rules explicitly. Surely, Frank was just being overly concerned about nothing. At least, he hoped that was the case.*

# CHAPTER TWENTY-THREE

TWO MONTHS LATER, SIX MONTHS SINCE LAUREL'S ACCIDENT.

During the last couple of months, Charles couldn't get Laurel out of his mind. He decided to go see her again. He could usually find her at the sidewalk cafe where he met her before without actually going to her apartment. It was early, before his practice was to begin. He casually walked down the street toward the cafe. As he neared the cafe he scanned over the people there hoping to see her. He stopped abruptly, as if he had been yanked from behind. There, sitting with Laurel, was Reece. A wave of jealousy washed over him. A feeling he was not expecting. They were talking and laughing. Charles turned suddenly so they wouldn't see him, and he hurriedly walked back to his office.

As he walked Charles became very concerned about his reaction. He had never felt this way about a woman before. He didn't know where the feelings were coming from. Nothing had prepared him for his reaction to seeing Laurel and Reece together. He only knew he had never really liked Reece. That was, also a feeling he didn't like. Disliking someone for no particular reason was a disgusting feeling that he would rather not have felt. He thought maybe his dislike for Reece was because Reece was a Spanner, who had decided to remain here, and become a part of *The Keeping Place* by becoming a Stayer. If that were the case, he should also dislike Laurel for being a Spanner, who might end up staying. He certainly did not dislike Laurel. As a matter-of-fact Charles liked Laurel more than he knew he should. She had been here quite awhile. Maybe she would stay. Until now, he hadn't realized that he had a problem.

The first time he had felt jealousy was when Reece had been talking with his best friend, Frank and his other friends. But, this was different. The magnitude of his feelings this time was almost overwhelming. Charles was beginning to hate Reece. He felt sick to his stomach by the time he reached his office. Guardians could occasionally have feelings of sickness, but it never went any farther than just being a discomforting sensation. He knew that it would pass soon. His office was filled with patients when he arrived. He put on his lab coat and began the daily routine of examining and counseling them. He would deal with his own emotions later. Right now his patients needed him.

Thinking back for a moment, Charles thought it funny that he would ever think that Laurel might stay. There were no indications that she would. *What*, he wondered, *would put that thought into his head?*

# CHAPTER TWENTY-FOUR

Laurel and Reece had been talking for about an hour when Reece jumped up and said he needed to get to his office. Laurel had gone down for breakfast and found Reece sitting at a table in the sidewalk cafe that she usually frequented.

She asked if she could join him, and he said, "Certainly. As a matter-of-fact, I was hoping I would see you this morning." They had seen quite a bit of each other, but it had been about a week since they had been together. They were becoming friends. Laurel seemed surprised at his candor, and wondered why he would want to see her on this particular morning.

"Why did you want to see me this morning?"

"Oh, it isn't anything important. I've missed you this past week, and I like talking to you. You're a pleasure to be around." She laughed at his obvious attempt to flirt with her. She was enjoying the attention he was giving her. They laughed and talked having a good time until he had to leave for work. She was sorry he had to go. She would have liked to spend more time with him this morning. She did have some things she was planning to do today, though. *Perhaps, it would be better to do them alone,* she thought.

They said their goodbyes and each went their separate ways, but not before Reece had set up a date to see her that evening. She liked Reece a lot, and she didn't mind the attention he was giving her. As long as she was going to be here, she might as well have a good time and enjoy good company. She didn't like being alone anyway. Although, today it was okay to be alone. She was going to go down the road by the cafe where she had come into this world and see what she could find. This time by herself. Maybe she would be able to find a way out of this place. At least, she would try. She wasn't going to spend much time there though, because she had a headache and felt kind of unusual. She wasn't sure what this feeling was. Maybe, she should go to see Charles later, after she got back. She would think about it, and see how the rest of the day went before she made any further decisions.

As Laurel left the sidewalk cafe, she thought she glimpsed Charles, but the person had hurried away so quickly that she wasn't sure if it had been him or not. She almost wished that it had been him. She had received a note on her door a few days before saying that the establishment she was living in wanted to move her to another building, and she wanted to find out why. She wondered why it wasn't her choice instead of theirs. After having been in the same building for six months, she didn't want to move. She had enough changes in her life right now, and an apartment change wasn't something she wanted to do. If they wanted to move her, she supposed they would do it whether she liked it or not.

Each day when she returned to her apartment building she expected them to tell her she had been moved. The note had indicated that the move would be to the building next door. Even though she couldn't understand why they would move her, she decided she would deal with it when it happened, instead of worrying about it now. Anyway, it would put her in the same building that Reece lived in. That wouldn't be so bad. She might even like that.

Laurel dismissed the idea that she may have seen Charles, thinking that if it had been him, he surely would have come over to join them since Reece was one of his associates at the clinic. It must have been someone who looked like him, she guessed. Heading out on her journey, she felt a rush of excitement at the thought of doing something that no one here knew she was doing. Most of the structures in town were all very close and within easy walking distance, but Nora's cafe was on the outskirts of the city, and a healthy walk. She had all day. It didn't matter how long it took.

Laurel started thinking of her life before all of this happened, while she walked. *What an odd turn of events,* she thought. A few months ago she was living the life she had always dreamed of with no apparent problems. It was a good life, and she missed it. She missed Kim, and the shop, and Kim's family. They had taken her in as if she had been another daughter to them.

Having lived in an orphanage most of her life, Laurel had always felt like an outsider until she met Kim. Kim's mother had died when Kim was in her teens. It had been a terrible time for her, and she turned to her father for the love and support that she needed. She became very close to her father, and visited him every day. Kim's family had become Laurel's family. They wrapped her in a warmth she had never felt before, but had needed so much. Laurel wanted to go back where she could feel that warmth again. And where she knew what was going on with people who cared for her. If only she could.

Something was missing from Laurel's life as she was growing up. She was sure that it must have been the feeling of unconditional love that comes from having a family. One question weighed heavily on her mind, though. *Why haven't they called me back?* She thought, *If they really loved me, would I still be here today? Or, would I be back where I belong, at home in my own world.* The thought that they didn't love her enough to call her back hurt her deeply.

Laurel walked on until she reached Nora's cafe. She didn't stop, but kept right on walking past the structure. She looked at the cafe all the while as she was passing it. Thinking, at any moment someone would walk out the door, but no one did. She just kept going. It took a long time to get past the cafe. She felt as if she were suspended in time. Again, a feeling that kept appearing throughout her stay here. Her legs seemed heavy. Her steps labored. It all seemed like a dream. Like she was pushing herself through a cloud. There were no sounds at all, except for the pounding in her ears.

Finally, after forcing herself to go on for more than an hour, Laurel realized she was getting nowhere. Feeling totally exhausted, she knelt down on the road with bended knees, placed her hands over her eyes and started sobbing. Each day her emotions surprised her, and she hadn't expected to feel like this. Then, something caught her eye, a shadow or something. She raised her head and looked down the road. She could see people coming down the road. All kinds of people. Men, women, and children. Passing her as if she weren't there. She stood up in stark amazement, not knowing what to do. She just stood there for several seconds, frozen, tears streaming down her face. Suddenly, she regained her senses, and she started to reach out to them. They just brushed past her like zombies. They just kept coming, and coming. She tried to talk to them, but with no response. As they continued to pass her she turned and watched them go. One by one, they kept going into Nora's cafe. Laurel started to follow the group of people, and as she approached the cafe, they all seemed to vanish. She walked into the cafe expecting to see all the people who had just past her. The dining room was empty. There was no one there.

A woman was standing behind the counter washing it off, completely oblivious to anything else that was happening around her.

Laurel quickly approached her and asked, "Where's Nora?"

"Oh! Hello, you startled me! May I help you?" she asked.

Laurel asked again, "Where's Nora?" Her voice was beginning to shake.

"I don't know anyone by that name. Was she supposed to meet you here or something?"

"What are you talking about?" Laurel screamed. "Nora runs this place!"

"I'm sorry," she said, calmly, "I don't know what you're talking about. I've been here for quite awhile, and I don't know anyone named Nora." She smiled and looked condescendingly at Laurel.

"That's impossible! Nora was here just a few days ago!" It had been two months ago, but to Laurel it had seemed like only a few days.

"Honey, you must be mistaken. Things do change quickly around here, but I do think I would remember if I wasn't here a few days ago. I know I haven't been appreciated like I should be, but that's a little weird," she said smiling to herself like Laurel was some kind of idiot. Laurel stumbled over to a booth by a window. She felt dizzy, and confused. She sat down and placed her head in her hands sobbing. The woman behind the counter walked over, and sat down across from her in the booth. She reached out and touched Laurel's arm, and tried to console her.

"Honey, I don't know where you came from or what you're

talking about, but I'm here to help you if I can. Would you like a drink or something?" At first, Laurel didn't...or couldn't say a word. Then, she looked up from her tears across the table at a face worn by years of hard living. Laurel must have looked crazy to this woman who seemed concerned about her.

"Can I get you something to drink?" she asked again. All Laurel could do was to nod her head. As the woman left to get the drink, Laurel tried to pull herself together, wiping her tears on a napkin. When the woman returned with the drink, Laurel thanked her, drank it down fast, and through her tears she started to explain what she was doing here.

"I just don't understand what's going on here. A few days ago Nora was here. We were talking about...about everything that's happening around here...and...and (she gestured with her hands)...the people...the people...everywhere...where are the people......I tried to touch...no one...would...The tears continued to flow.

For a moment she was becoming hysterical again, and then, she said with slurred words, "I'm getting very...tired. I think...I'll just...rest here...at the table...for a...." Those were the last words she spoke as she leaned forward onto the table and slipped into a peaceful sleep.

# CHAPTER TWENTY-FIVE

ONE YEAR SINCE THE ACCIDENT

It was after hours and Dr. James Martin was calling Kim Donalson to talk again about whether or not she would ever make a decision to take Laurel Richards off life support. He had a more than usual interest in Ms. Richards's case. Perhaps, because his own brother Reece was in a coma at the present time. He had never mentioned that to Kim, or anyone else for that matter. The only people who knew about it were the staff at the hospital, his closest friends and his family.

James and his brother were only a year apart in age, and looked so much alike that some people would mistake them for twins. James' hair was a little darker than Reece's, and they both had such strikingly beautiful blue eyes that everyone would notice them at first glance. They had done everything together. They had even spent time in medical school together. James, being the older of the two, had been accepted first. Then, a year later Reece had come into the same school. They both graduated with honors. They had always been very competitive, but then, something had happened to Reece. He had gotten in with the wrong crowd, the wild life, and had started taking drugs, mind altering drugs. He had gone into paranoia at times, and bordered on schizophrenic behavior. As hard as they, James and his parents, had tried, they still lost him. Reece had eventually taken an overdose and was currently in a coma.

James and his parents had thought maybe it would be a blessing for Reece to die. He was not on any kind of life support, but he continued to live. It had been a terrible thing for James to handle. He felt like he had lost half of himself. He tried so hard to help his brother get off the drugs. So hard, in fact, that Reece, being upset with the interventions had alienated himself from the family, saying that he had no family. He had been delusional most of the time before he overdosed.

Their father had been an alcoholic which proved there was obsessive behavior in the family prior to Reece's problem. This weighed heavily over their father's head, and he committed suicide a year later. Their father felt totally to blame for Reece's condition, as any parent might. Although, the ultimate responsibility lay with Reece. He had made his own choices. Reece thought he could handle the drugs, but he became addicted almost immediately. A few times he tried to quit, but he always gave in to the weakness again. He was never quite strong enough to resist the control they had on his mind and body, subsequently destroying his mind or, so everyone thought.

Reece had been in a coma for more than two years. The medical profession doesn't know much about comas. Perhaps, he was still in there, in his mind trying to get out, healing. James could only hope, and pray.

Now, not only had James lost the brother he adored to this medical condition, but he had lost his father too. He had never been really close to his father, but there is still that feeling of losing something deep down inside of yourself that somehow keeps you whole. *Maybe it's that connection that makes you feel like you belong in this world,* he thought. Losing a parent gives a person the feeling that this connection with life has been lost. Sometimes he wondered how he kept going—doing his daily tasks, but he tried to be strong for his mother's sake at least. His work at the hospital was what kept his mind off his personal problems. He enjoyed being able to take care of people in need. He saw his brother every day at the Care Center, but he was able to remove himself from the pain when he left the room. As he left the building, some overriding power would intervene, making him feel that he must keep going, and never give up.

James wanted to talk to Kim to get this thing settled. Laurel lay in that bed hooked to those life support tubes, and as far as James was concerned, they were doing her no good at all. She was still in a state of rigidity where her arms were bent at the elbows, and her hands and fists were clenched tightly against her chest. There had been some spasticity (uncontrolled movement), but not enough to be considered actual movement.

When they realized that Laurel wasn't going to come out of the coma, they placed her in a hoisted frame from the ceiling to make it easier for the nurses to turn her from her back to her front, which was done daily to prevent bedsores. Physical therapy had been provided, but it was minimal. Because of the spasticity and the tremendous rigidity produced by the brain, the therapy was relatively useless in preventing the joints from becoming tight. James felt there wasn't enough being done to try and stimulate coma patients. It was his hope that possibly the shock of removing the support system would awaken his patient. It was a theory that he had hoped would work, although it had not worked with Reece.

James dialed the phone number. It rung several times. When he was about to hang up a pleasant voice answered.

"Hello," Kim said. She had been dozing at the kitchen table. She was trying to straighten out the myriad of paperwork involved with running a business. It had been piling up, and she had been bringing the paperwork home each night. Tonight, she just couldn't seem to keep her mind on it long enough to get through it. Laurel had done most of the office work, but now, it was up to Kim to handle it, as was everything else. Kim had been the creative one. She had been the fun loving spirit that had started the whole thing, and she was becoming weighed down with the tediousness, and the absolute boredom associated with paperwork.

Along with buying the products, and running the store completely by herself, it was almost enough to overwhelm her when each night she had to come home to this. She was totally exhausted from working all day and then working half the night. She welcomed the call. Anything to break the monotony. She tried to sound like she hadn't been dozing. She had been successful. Dr. Martin hadn't suspected a thing.

"Kim, it's James. I was wondering if you are ready to make the decision to take Laurel off life support. You know, it's been a year now."

"Well, yes" she said hesitantly, "I have thought about it…a lot,

actually. I know I've avoided making this decision for long enough."
She knew the time had come for her to finally face reality, and she
needed to talk to him. "I want to come down and talk to you in person.
I don't think a decision like this should be made over the phone."
Kim had waited as long as she could to face the situation.

After the first four months Kim had almost decided to remove the
support system, but then after a heart wrenching struggle, she
changed her mind. James had kept trying to reason with her. He was
very persistent, and Kim almost hardened herself against his ideas.
She hadn't wanted to confront her own fears. But now, she felt she
must do something. She had tried to keep herself so busy that she
wouldn't have to make this decision, and she had almost succeeded,
but James had hounded her about it every few weeks. Now, she felt
she should at least give him the time to present his case. She had
never really listened to his theories. In her heart she knew what
would be best for Laurel, but her head kept fighting the decisions that
needed to be made because it was too difficult for her to bear. In her
mind, if she didn't deal with the situation she could avoid the feelings
of responsibility that deep down made her feel weak and inadequate,
and ultimately unable to make the decision that James wanted her to
make.

After six months, they had moved Laurel to the Care Center into
*Room 204*, where she was under 24 hour care. James wanted to
remove the life support then, but Kim just wouldn't deal with it,
again. The move had not been easy on Laurel, and she had appeared
to be under stress.

After waiting for her to stabilize, Kim found another excuse for
not removing the support system. And since then, the time just
seemed to slip away. The more time that passed, the more removed
from the situation she became. The busier she became, the less time
she had to visit Laurel. Therefore, she could justify all the hours she
was spending at work. Thus, justifying the lack of time she was
spending with Laurel. She was only visiting her every two weeks at
present, and if something came up she would miss that visit too. It
was almost as if putting her in the care center had relieved Kim of any

responsibility.

Now, it seemed that Dr. Martin was forcing the issue. Now, it had been exactly a year, and she would not be able to put him off any longer. She did want to see him, and she hadn't wanted to haggle over the time, but it would have to be after hours. She had no one to look after the shop if she were to leave during the daytime. She had exhausted any help that was available at first. People have their own lives to live, and you can only ask so much of them.

When Kim was a little girl, and into her teens, her mother had always been there for her when she needed help. When her mother died, Kim felt like the bottom had fallen out of her world. Her Father had been there for her, but a girl needs her mother. Perhaps, that was one reason she and Laurel had hit it off so well. They both needed someone and they were, to each other, that person.

James understood Kim's situation, and had agreed to meet with her at 7:00 the next evening. They would meet in the lobby of the care center next to the hospital. He would be working late that evening. He thought it would the logical place to meet.

# CHAPTER TWENTY-SIX

Laurel awoke with a start. She was lying on a bed in a room that looked like a hospital room. Everything was white. The sheets, the walls, the ceilings…everything was pure white. A red light was flashing above her door, and suddenly Dr. Statten, Charles, appeared through the door. "Well, you finally decided to wake up I see," he said cheerily. She wasted no time in getting right to the point, although she felt a little groggy.

"What's going on here?" she asked weakly. Why am I here? I was at Nora's cafe and…."

"What were you doing there?" he asked abruptly, interrupting her.

Regaining her angry disposition she demanded, "What is this? An interrogation? And, besides that, it isn't Nora's place anymore. There's some other person there. Where's Nora?"

"That's not important right now. I want to know what you thought you were doing there in the first place," he insisted.

"Not important to whom?" she yelled back at him. "You have no right telling me where I can or cannot go!"

"Please, I don't mean to upset you," he apologized. "You have been through another ordeal that I wish you had not put yourself through. If you'll just calm down, I'll try to explain everything to you."

"Well, you had better. I'm getting pretty tired of all this intrigue. It looks like you're all trying to conspire against me."

"No one is conspiring against anyone here. You place yourself into these precarious situations that require drastic steps to correct. We are only doing our jobs, and you are making it very difficult for everyone concerned. It would help if you would cooperate a little," She was feeling exasperated. She wasn't getting the answers she wanted, and she was feeling confused and scared.

"I would like to cooperate if I could get all the answers."

"Nobody knows all the answers. Did you know absolutely everything in your world before you came here?"

Before she could answer, he added, "Of course, you didn't. It's impossible to know everything all the time. We haven't given you all the facts, because most people can't handle the whole truth all at once, and that apparently applies to you. We gave you all the details we felt you needed to know at the time. As time goes on, we would have given you more details, and we still will, but you have to be patient. Sometimes we don't tell you something just because it hasn't come up yet. And when it does, we will fill you in on the details." She started to talk and he raised his hand to shush her. He needed to get these things said without any interruptions.

"Remember when you first came, I told you that you would be given the information you needed, as you needed it?" She nodded. "Well, we are still doing that. You are given whatever you need for your well being. What you did by going to the place where you entered this world was not beneficial to you. You actually caused yourself harm. Notice the date on the wall calendar," he said. She hadn't noticed that there was a calendar before, but she looked over at it hanging on the wall amid the whiteness. She got off the bed, holding her gown with one hand behind her. She walked up and looked closely at the date. Her mouth fell open and she raised her free hand to cover her mouth. The date on the calendar said it was not the date that she had known it was yesterday, but it was six months later. She had been here a whole year. All that time had passed since yesterday. Six months had passed since her trip down the road.

She said, after she had regained her composure, "You're trying to trick me aren't you? This isn't real, it can't be!"

He said, "Oh, it's real alright. Your time here had to be extended purposely to get you under control."

"That's not possible! You can't do this to me!" she gasped.

"Yes, we can, and we did." he said calmly. "But, not for the reasons you're thinking. We had to do it for your health. You were out of control, and would have been of no good to anyone, including yourself, in that state of mind. If you had been taken back at that time, you might have suffered brain damage. We saved you from that. We, *and you*, were lucky that it wasn't your time to go back. There are times when people have slipped back through with stunts like this one you just pulled, before they are ready, before they have made that crucial decision, and they almost all...95% at least, suffer some kind of brain damage, and are never able to fully recover from their comatose state. We intervene whenever possible to stop that from happening."

"I...I didn't know," she stuttered.

"Of course, you didn't know. That was one of the things we didn't think we would need to tell you. You were not ready to return. I can see right now that we need to sit you down and tell you everything that might enter that head of yours before you cause yourself any more harm," he said. "I want you to come to my office everyday for the next few weeks so I can explain all of this to you in great detail, okay?" She reluctantly agreed.

"You get dressed, and I'll see to your release this afternoon. Oh, by-the-way, he said," very matter-of-factly, like it had no bearing on anything, "your apartment building has been changed. You are in the building directly west of the building you were previously in. You are now in *Room 204*. Someone else has been placed in your former room." As he left the room he smiled like nothing at all had happened. Trying to make her realize he wasn't quite the ogre that he felt she must be thinking he was.

Charles decided that he had probably come on a little too strongly to her. She took the smile to be an attempt at covering for his particularly bad behavior, after he had lashed out at her so cruelly. She had a hard time reading him. She always wondered what his intentions really were. Sometimes, he was very friendly, and then another time he would seem like a complete jerk. Today, he hadn't helped her opinion of him in the least. Maybe, he could forget about his attitude toward her a few minutes ago, but she couldn't. She was mad, and she wouldn't get over it easily even though, she had seen a kinder, gentler side of him when they had walked to Nora's cafe on that day a few months ago.

She wondered how the time had slipped away. *Had they kept her drugged all that time? For six months? How was it possible for a whole year to have passed since she first came here?* Her mind just couldn't comprehend such a thing. *Was it beneficial to her well being as they kept telling her? She guessed she would never know the answer to that question.*

While she dressed she started planning her next move all the while talking to herself, asking herself aloud, "Who does he think he is? Treating me like that! I'll show him who can be controlled, and who cannot!" She would be more careful in the future. She didn't want to stay here longer than was absolutely necessary, and she would determine the proper way to find out things the next time. Because, there *would be* a next time. She wasn't going to sit around, and simply wait for her time to come to leave. She would be ready to go, and she wanted to know how to do it the right way. She would attend each meeting she was supposed to. She would play his little game, and would observe everything around her.

Now, Laurel was wondering, *Did they have some ulterior motive for moving me to another room? Why would they do that?* She knew they planned to move her because of the note someone had left on her door. *But, did they really need the other room for someone else? And, why did they need to do it right now,* she wondered? *Why couldn't they have given this Room 204 to the new person?* It didn't make any sense to her at all. She hadn't been all that attached to her former room. Maybe it didn't matter. At this point in time, a different room had no bearing on what her future might hold. She didn't plan on staying much longer. It made no real difference to her. She shook her head and thought, *I can't believe I've had been here this long.* She would try hard not to do anything that might extend her stay any longer than it had already been. A year of her life, lost.

She was really beginning to feel trapped. She needed to see Reece. She wondered if he were still here. The thought of the only person she felt close to being gone was almost more than she could bear. As soon as she was allowed to leave this hospital she would try to find him.

# CHAPTER TWENTY-SEVEN

Kim was finishing up at the store. Doing the last minute things to close up when James walked through the door. Kim was more than surprised. Shock would best fit the description of her feelings.

Without waiting to hear any explanation he might have, Kim asked very bluntly, "What are you doing here? I thought we were supposed to meet at the Care Center." James was a little taken aback from her reaction. He had decided to pick her up and escort her to the Center thinking it would make a more relaxed atmosphere. Maybe, give them a chance to ease the tension of the situation.

"I guess I should have called," he said rather sheepishly.

"You guess?"

"I just thought it might give us a few minutes to talk about something other than the problem at hand. But, you're absolutely right, I messed up, and I'm sorry. If I leave right now I can probably still meet you at the appointed time, and we can pretend I was never here," he said, trying to lighten up the situation with a bit of humor.

"No, No…It's alright…now that you're here," she said, acting like she had missed the humor of his remark. "Let me finish closing the store. I'll be ready in a few minutes." She scurried around putting the cash drawer in the safe and locking the stock room door that led to the outside of the building. Actually, she was pleased by his unexpected appearance, and found it hard not to smile. She found him to be very attractive and comfortable to be with, but she wasn't going to let him know how she felt. She was surprised by her reaction to his sudden appearance since she had previously felt no emotions toward him at all. At least, any emotions she would let herself recognize. Her emotional state was anything but normal at the present time.

Kim had planned to spend a few minutes re-doing her makeup and hair before she left the shop but now, she would have to go as she was. Even without makeup she was a beautiful woman. There wasn't anything that really needed doing. Her beauty had not gone unnoticed by James. Both she and Laurel were very striking. When walking down the streets of the city together, many heads would turn at the sight of them.

James had asked the taxi driver to park in front of the shop, and wait for him. He glanced out at the cab several times, while he looked around at the various items in the shop, making sure that it was still there. He wasn't really interested in the things in the shop, but he was impressed with her selection of the unusual. He could see she had a knack for her chosen profession.

The weather was turning cool. James was dressed in a long black top coat with a soft gray scarf wrapped around his neck. Kim had left the room, but now she was back carrying her coat on one arm. James helped her with her coat. Then, he reached for the door, opened it, and stood back while she locked the door. He stood there, almost in a trance, overwhelmed with her beauty. She spoke, bringing him back to the moment in an instant,

"You know, I'm actually glad that you came to pick me up. I dread driving through the city at this time of night. The traffic is so heavy, and I have had a hard time handling it since Laurel's accident. I take a bus or a taxi to most places I need to go to now. As a matter-of-fact I haven't had my car out of the garage for a week. I live close enough to the shop to walk. Unless I feel the need to visit my father, I don't drive much at all."

James smiled at her and said, "I know what you're saying. As you can see, I too came in a taxi. I don't even own a car." She seemed to be relaxing which was just what he had intended this trip to accomplish. He needed her to realize that he was not the bad guy. He only wanted what would be best for Laurel, and taking her off life support at this point in time would be, in his estimation, the right thing to do.

During the ride they talked about the weather, the stock market which he was surprised that she was so knowledgeable about, and what the St. Louis Cardinals would be doing this next season. When the taxi turned into the parking lot of the Care Center they both became very somber. The time had come to face reality. The jovial attitude that had been present only minutes before had changed. She had a better feeling about James now though, and she had begun to think he might really be a nice guy after all. Kim had never quite understood why he was so relentless about removing Laurel from life support. She wondered if he really thought it would help Laurel stay alive. His motives weren't exactly clear, but he did seem sincere.

After they stopped in front of the Care Center, the cab driver opened the door, and Kim stepped out. James went out the opposite door, and hurried around to walk with Kim up to the front door. As they walked up to the Center James took Kim's arm, as if assisting her.

Kim was moved by his thoughtful demeanor, but pulled away saying, "I can walk by myself, thank you." James looked surprised at her attitude, but he said nothing. He thought he understood her feelings at the moment, and would try to be more compassionate. He was also beginning to realize that there was a lot of unresolved anger in this person, and thought he would be more careful when approaching her. The night watchman had locked the front doors. James pulled out his keys and unlocked them. The night staffers were on duty taking care of the patients, and doing whatever was needed. There was always a registered nurse on duty, and a receptionist.

As they passed the receptionist's desk she greeted James. "Hello, Dr. Martin. Working late again, as usual?"

"Yes, but only for a little while tonight. Helen, this is Ms. Kim Donalson. We're here to discuss a patient of mine. We won't be here long." The two women nodded to each other and smiled.

"We'll see you later," James said, as they walked on down the corridor. "We have a very qualified staff here as I'm sure you already know. Any of them can be called in case of an emergency at any time of the day or night. We pride ourselves in being the best Care Center in the state," he said.

"I am very much aware of the care Laurel has been receiving since we put her here." Kim added sarcastically, feeling guilty about her passive attitude during the past few months, "But, thank you for reminding me of what a great place this is." Changing the subject she asked, "Do you have an office in this building too?"

"Well, we do a kind of a sharing thing here with all the doctors using the same office. Usually, there is only one doctor here at a time. Especially, since there are always doctors available at the hospital across the street. This is not a large building as you can see, and we need all the space for patients." They stopped in front of a door at the end of the hall. James pulled out his keys and unlocked the door. Opening the door with one hand and leaning across the opening, he switched on the light. It was the typical doctor's office, the big desk, the two soft overstuffed chairs just like at the hospital. He asked Kim to be seated in one of the chairs as he walked around the desk and seated himself behind it. There was a sudden silence in the room. They both looked at each other. Neither one wanting to make the first move.

But then, James started by saying, "I think we should get right to the point. As you know, I have recommended several times that you take Laurel off life support. It's my opinion that it may trigger something in her brain that could possibly bring her back. But, it's only a theory. I do not feel that it would…or could cause her any harm. She appears to be in excellent physical condition at this time. All of the physical disabilities that she sustained in the accident have healed very well."

"Why is it so important to you that we do this right now?" Kim asked.

"The longer we wait…" he paused… "If we wait longer…there could be some deterioration to her bodily functions. We have already noticed some changes." He was being careful not to upset Kim, trying to choose just the right words to use. My main concern is her health. She is as healthy as she will ever be right now."

"I can see that these are important reasons to do this for Laurel's sake, but you still haven't answered my question about your interest in this case." Kim insisted. James hadn't wanted to suggest that he had any personal interest in this case, but maybe it would help Kim to understand his motives.

"I wouldn't have told you this, but since you asked, I'll tell you. I probably have more than a usual interest. Not necessarily because of the patient involved, although I do have compassion for all my patients. It's more about the case itself. My brother, like your friend Laurel, is also in a coma. In this very facility." Kim was astonished at this revelation, but went on with her questioning as if it meant nothing to her. She felt a small amount of compassion for him, but she wasn't going to accept any more sadness in her life. She had her own to deal with, and that was enough.

"What does this have to do with Laurel?"

"Nothing, other than to help you understand my interest in coma patients. I've had to personally deal with the same things you are dealing with right now. It was terribly hard to remove Reece from life support, but professionally, I have felt that sometimes the shock of removing the life support may bring a coma patient back to life, to reality. It does happen sometimes."

"Apparently, it didn't work with your brother or he wouldn't still be in a coma. Is that right?" Kim suddenly became annoyed with the thought that he was willing to subject her friend to danger because of his personal motives. *Trial and error*, she thought.

"Yes, that is right, it didn't work for Reece, but, I have seen it happen with other patients. This isn't something that just popped into my head. I have experienced dramatic results with other patients, and I feel it's worth the risk. I felt it was worth the risk with my own brother. As you can probably imagine, I was heartsick when it failed to bring Reece back through *The Veil*. We were very close," he said, lowering his eyes to the desk. He paused for a moment. Kim felt embarrassed about her lack of concern for James' feelings. Kim had so many emotions going on in her head about her own personal feelings that she sometimes forgot there were other people suffering through as much turmoil as she.

Bringing herself back to the conversation with a question she asked, "What do you mean, 'back through *The Veil?*'"

"It doesn't mean anything. I've often wondered where the mind goes when a person is in a coma. I guess I was just thinking out loud."

"I've never really thought about it that way," Kim said. "It certainly is an unusual concept to think that the mind is actually somewhere else. I just assumed that the mind was totally blank, like it was resting with no thoughts at all."

"Wouldn't you like to think that it would be better if there were somewhere else for the mind to go? Instead of sitting there in a vegetative state?" He could see he was losing her so he continued quickly past that part of the conversation, "It's just a thought. Probably a silly one at that. Reece has been in a coma long enough for me to have had all kinds of thoughts. Even…apparently silly ones. I've sat by his bedside for many hours, and wondered where his mind is, or if he even has a mind left. His coma was induced by a drug overdose. We will never be sure, until he either wakes up…or….," He stopped, not wanting to say the word that he most dreaded.

He continued, "We do know that he still has some active brain waves. To what extent they are still normal, only time will tell. In the meantime, I would like to think he is someplace where he's happy. Hopefully, happier than he was when he was here with us."

"How long has he been in a coma?"

"It's been almost three years," he said quietly. "Enough about my problems. I think we should get on with why we came here tonight. Your friend, Laurel needs your help now. I know it's risky, but don't you think it's worth the risk to try to bring her back? As far as I am concerned, personally, I would be willing to try anything to bring someone I cared about out of a coma, no matter what it takes." Kim looked down at her hands which were clasped tightly in her lap.

"You may think that I have taken too long to make this decision, but I don't think you realize the position this has put me in. Laurel is my friend, but to decide, whether she is to live or die, is a tremendous responsibility for me to take. If she were a blood relative I think it might be easier. What if she were to die when the machines are taken away? I would feel like I had killed her, myself. I alone would be responsible," she emphasized this by placing her hand on her chest. Tears welled up in her eyes as she spoke.

James said calmly with compassion, "Try to think of it this way.

You would be taking responsibility for giving her a chance for life rather than taking her life away. I am sure that Laurel would want you to make this decision on her behalf knowing that you would not do anything to harm her." Kim wiped away the tears that were streaming down her face.

"When you say it like that, it doesn't seem so wrong," She straightened herself in the chair, took a deep breath, and said, "Alright, I'll do it. But, I need a few more days to get my mind ready for whatever the outcome may be."

"That's fine. It will take a few days to get everything ready anyway. I'll contact you when we have the staff ready, and then you can let me know exactly when you *will* be ready. Let me tell you this, it's no easier if it is a blood relative. That may make it even harder. I know. I don't think you will be sorry, Kim." With a smile on his face he reached across the desk to take Kim's hand. Kim stood, extended her hand, and returned the smile. As they left the room, and walked down the hall James said he would have the receptionist call a cab for her return home. He intended to remain in the Center awhile longer. He wanted to visit Reece tonight before he returned home. Kim told him it would not be necessary for him to call a cab for her now because she was going to visit Laurel before she left, and she would call a cab later when she was ready to leave. James left her in the corridor with the comment that he would see her in a few days, and he returned to his office.

James felt relieved that Kim had finally made the decision he felt was right. The decision that might bring her friend back to life. He had hope for awhile, and he wanted to share this feeling with someone, and the only person he had was Reece. Of course, he had his mother, but it was hard to talk to her about these things. It would make her sad if she had to re-live the idea that this same procedure had not worked with Reece, and James didn't want to remind her of that each time he had a patient in the same situation. He had tried to talk to her at first, but he could see how it affected her. He decided not to mention it all. Now, he would talk to Reece, but was never sure if he were actually there. Sharing this and other things with Reece was the only way he knew how to try and keep his brother real. *If only this procedure had worked for Reece,* he thought as he re-entered his office to finish some paperwork before he went to visit him.

James wanted to make sure that everything was ready when the time came for the removal of the life support system from Laurel. There were forms to fill out, and papers to sign. It would take some extra hours to finish his portion of the paperwork. He would have everything ready as soon as possible.

Kim walked down the hall to the elevators. She pushed the up button. The elevator was already on the first floor. The door opened almost instantly. She stepped into the elevator and pushed the floor number. When the elevator stopped on the second floor the doors opened and Kim stepped through them into the corridor with a sigh. *Do I really want to be here,* she thought. *No, I really don't, but I have no choice.* She needed to talk this out with Laurel, even though laurel probably wouldn't even know she was here…to let her know what they were about to do.

As Kim entered Laurel's room, she walked over to the bed and gazed down on the person in the bed. Was this really Laurel, or was there anyone in there, inside this motionless body lying there. It seemed so long ago that this person had been a vibrant, happy person living life to the fullest. She thought, *What a tragic twist of fate this has been. Laurel has always had to work so hard to have even the semblance of a normal life and now look what has happened to her.*

All of Laurel's determination had been wasted as far as Kim could see, but on the other hand, maybe that determination was keeping her alive. It made her sad to see Laurel like this. She didn't intend to stay very long. She looked over Laurel with the feeding tubes in her nose. There were needles inserted in her wrists and held in place with surgical tape to keep her body filled with the right amount of fluids. She looked at the machines buzzing and whirring and thought, *This is no way to live.* She felt she had made the right decision. Soon, they would know, one way or another, if it were the right decision for Laurel. It had been a tough decision to make, but now after considering what James had said, she could see it was the only way. She felt guilty for feeling this way, but she thought that if taking the life support off didn't bring Laurel out of the coma, and she couldn't function without it, maybe it would be better...if she...died.

# CHAPTER TWENTY-EIGHT

Laurel had been released from the place that appeared to be a hospital. She walked out into the sunshine. Everything was beautiful. The air around her felt almost soft on her skin. The scenery practically exploded around her. The trees were the greenest of greens with hues of bright yellow and orange. The grass was like a cushion under her feet. She looked up at the houses and buildings that were vibrant with color, and so clean. It was like looking at a picture postcard. She had almost forgotten how beautiful it was. It was hard to think that anyone would ever want to leave a place so absolutely perfect.

Laurel smiled as a warm feeling of awareness of life, and everything around her almost overwhelmed her. That was when she realized what was wrong. *It's so perfect here that no one wants to leave. They are lulled into thinking this place is a paradise, and they sit back and do nothing. That's why people seem so happy here,* she thought. She felt like she had stumbled onto a secret that no one else had ever thought of. *They couldn't know this, or they would be doing something to get out of here,* she believed. She headed straight for Charles' office where she was going to confront him with what she had just discovered. She was not going to wait until tomorrow to straighten this out. As she walked down the street she found it hard to keep her resolve.

This feeling of well being was so hard to resist that she had to fully concentrate on her objective in order to keep mind focused. She had experienced this same feeling right after she had arrived here, and she remembered how it had almost engulfed her then. By the time she reached Charles' office, it was all she could do to remember why she had come, but she hung onto her thoughts with a determination that would have challenged any lesser person's resolve.

Charles was sitting at his desk when Laurel entered his office.

The receptionist had notified Charles that Laurel was on her way to his office.

"Come in, Laurel. I didn't expect to see you so soon."

"I'm sure you didn't!" she said sharply. Being inside a building seems to soften the effects of the "Rosy Exposure" as she had resorted to calling it.

"Please sit down, and we can talk about whatever seems to be bothering you," he said calmly.

"Alright," she said, as she walked around and seated herself in one of the chairs in front of his desk. She sat there for a few minutes glaring at Charles. Trying to get a feeling of just what this man had to do with this deception. Was he the mastermind behind this charade, or just a puppet for some higher authority? She needed to know. How could he seem this sincere, when she felt there was something, not necessarily evil, but morally unjust about everything?

She began, "I have been noticing how pleasant everything is around here. The weather, the scenery, the houses. It seems to have the effect of putting people into an ambrosial state of mind that keeps them under control."

"I see," he said. "You have finally found us out." He had to cover his mouth to hide a smile that was creeping through. "I don't know what you think you have discovered, but you couldn't be more wrong. I don't know why you think you must continue to fight us on everything we do. I've told you before that we are here to help you. Why can't you just accept that?"

"What!" she exclaimed. "Accept the fact that you want us to act like cattle? To accept every little thing that you tell us? To walk around like zombies, and never try to be an individual?"

"I'm sorry that you feel that way. That has not been our intent at all, although, it may seem that way to someone on the outside."

"Am I on the outside?"

"Yes, you are, actually. Most people who come here are here and gone in a few days. A few months at the most. There are a few of you who are here longer, and to them, and to you, it may seem that there is some deception going on. There really isn't. We just try to make your stay here as pleasant as we can until you decide what you are going to do. It really is up to you whether you stay or leave, but somehow you haven't made that decision."

"I think I have!" she said emphatically.

"No, you really haven't. Somewhere, in your mind, there is something keeping you from making that decision fully. You may think you have, but if you had, you wouldn't still be here. Your body is, apparently, fully recovered from the accident you had a year ago. Your mind seems to be sound as well. You think we are keeping you here, but in reality it is you who is having a hard time making the decision to leave." Laurel was stunned. She didn't know how to react to that revelation. She sat there staring at him wondering if this were just another way of trying to keep her under control until they could decide what to do with her.

He said, "Go to your apartment and think about this some more. I would like to see you tomorrow. Can we arrange a meeting after I finish my rounds at the clinic?" She stood up feeling like she had just lost a battle with the Devil. Although he seemed sincere, she just didn't know whether she should believe him.

"Yes, I'll be free," she said, only half thinking about what he had said about meeting him. *Of course, she would be free. She didn't have a thing in this world to do, but to sit and wait for whatever was going to happen next.* Her mind was muddled trying to think of any possible reason why she would not make a mental decision to leave this place. *Was this what he was trying to do, confuse her?* If that were the case, it had worked. She felt as if she had been knocked to the floor, and couldn't get up.

Laurel walked to her apartment in a daze. As she approached the building where she had lived for the past few months, she remembered that they had moved her to the next apartment complex. She entered the building, noticing that it looked the same as the one she had been in before. The desk clerk even had a similar look. She was too confused to think any more about that. She decided that even though there was an elevator she would take the stairs to her new room. It was only on the second floor.

As she rounded the second flight of stairs, and started down the hall to *Room 204*, Laurel could see someone leaning on the wall with his head hung down looking at the floor. It was Reece. She couldn't believe the feeling of elation coming over her just by seeing this man, this friend. She almost ran down the hall. He looked up and greeted her with the biggest smile he could muster, and ran to meet her down the corridor. Laurel threw herself into his waiting arms. They embraced for a long time. Neither of them knowing what to say to each other. The lingering embrace felt so comforting that Laurel didn't want to let go. This was a feeling that she had needed. Before now, the fear and confusion hadn't let her feel anything at all. She felt completely relaxed in his arms. She wanted to stay there forever, and forget about everything else.

She finally looked up into his eyes and said with a smile, "Hi! I'm glad to see you." As if the dam had been broken, the tears started flowing down her cheeks.

Reece was crying too, as he said, "I thought you had gone away. I looked for you, but I couldn't find you, and then Charles told me what had happened, but he didn't tell me where you had been taken." He gently wiped away the tears from her face with his thumb while still holding her close to him. "Where have you been? What's the matter? I've never seen you this upset."

She pulled away slowly, and in a dejected voice said, "Oh, nothing, everything!" waving her hands in the air pathetically.

"Do you know how long I've been gone? To me it seems like just a day, but in reality it has been six months in our world time. I don't understand what's happening to me. I just don't know what to do anymore. I've always been in complete control of my life until now. I feel lost in a world where I have no control over my own destiny!" She pulled a tissue from her pocket and wiped her nose, and dabbed at her eyes.

"It seems so hopeless. Everything I try to do seems to backfire!" she said, as she sat down next to the wall and pulled up her knees. She wrapped her arms around her knees and slumped down over them.

Reece sat down in the middle of the hall right in front of her and placed his hand on one of her knees.

Then he lifted her chin and said tenderly, "Hey, it's not that bad. Things have to get better. They always do. Anyway, what has brought on this barrage of sad feelings? This isn't the feisty girl I've come to know and...love." She looked into his eyes, those beautiful blue eyes that almost seemed transparent, and that gentle face, and she knew at that moment she had very strong feelings for this man. He leaned closer and gently kissed her on the lips. She returned the kiss with more passion than she knew she had within herself. She was falling in love with him, and right now she wasn't in a state of mind to stop it.

Reece stood up and pulled Laurel to her feet. She turned and opened the door to her apartment. He lifted her into his arms and carried her to the bed where they consummated their love, and for awhile Laurel was able to forget about the worries of the world around her. She felt whole again. They felt no guilt because when two people truly love each other there is no closer bond. And with that, there is no sin in this world or any other. When the Man from Elysian Fields looks down and sees love, and feels love, all is well in the worlds he has created.

# CHAPTER TWENTY-NINE

Laurel didn't stir until the sun filtering through the curtains shone on her face. She reached over to touch Reece, but he was already gone. She felt an emptiness surround her. She called out his name, but he had left the apartment. She went into the bathroom, and noticed that the shower was dry. *He must have left during the night*, she thought. She showered and dressed, and decided to take a walk. She was thinking about what she should do with herself if she were never able to leave this place. Since her liaison with Reece, Laurel felt better about being here, even though *staying here*, in her conscious mind, was not an option.

Charles had said, that it was her choice whether she wanted to leave, or not. She couldn't believe he was telling her the truth. She was convinced that if it really were her choice, she would have been gone by now. She had absolutely no doubts about this feeling. She felt like they were trying to keep her here for some reason. She would still try to find a way to leave, but in the mean time she might as well keep herself busy. Maybe, she should seek out the children. Charles had said that she could see them if she wanted to. Still mulling these things around in her mind, she quickly left her apartment.

Laurel was just leaving the building when she saw Charles just ahead of her. Almost as if it had been planned. That thought only breezed past her mind momentarily as she hurried to catch up to him. "Rosy Exposure" was setting in again, but she let it pass through her conscious mind, and into her subconscious mind with little thought of the subtle conditioning she was receiving. Charles seemed pleased to have her company. He asked her to join him for breakfast, and she gladly agreed.

"You seem to be in a better frame of mind this morning than you did yesterday afternoon," he said.

"You're right, Doctor. I feel much better today. As a matter-of-fact, I would like to see the children. Remember you once said I could see them if I wanted to?"

"Yes, I do recall that conversation. When would you like to see them?"

"Right away, if you don't mind," she said with enthusiasm. There was an urgency in her mind that she really didn't understand, but she felt it important not to waste time. She was almost driven by a need to get things done. Charles said he would have to make arrangements, but thought they could probably go this afternoon.

When Charles and Laurel reached the sidewalk cafe, a few people were seated at tables. Several of them nodded to Charles, and he acknowledged them with a smile as he pulled out a chair for Laurel. She was surprised that there was any interaction with these people because previously she had seen none. After they were seated the waiter came to take their orders.

"Well, good morning Dr. Statten." the waiter said.

"Good morning, Victor, how are you today?"

"Couldn't be better. Do you want your usual?"

"No, this morning I'll just have coffee, but Ms. Richards may want something." Laurel was surprised with all this cordiality, but she just ordered a cup of tea and said nothing. She was delighted that Charles could make arrangements to see the children so soon, and she wasn't going to let anything upset her. She had been afraid he would say it would take a few days, and she wouldn't have been willing to wait, although she wasn't sure why. They talked for awhile and then Charles left to take care of his practice, and to make whatever arrangements he needed for their visit to see the children. Charles said he would contact her at her apartment as soon as he could find out what time they could visit the children.

Since Laurel had some time to kill, she decided she would see if she could find Reece. *He must have gone to work*, she thought. She left the cafe and walked down the street admiring her surroundings. She had almost reached the park when she thought she saw Reece enter through the gates. She hurried as fast as she could, but he was gone by the time she arrived. She looked around, but couldn't see which direction he had taken. She wondered if she could enter through the gates, as he had. Remembering how she had been knocked down from some kind of unseen force before, she wasn't eager to try that again. She carefully placed her hands in front of herself and began feeling around to see if she could actually enter the park. As before, she could feel there was something there preventing her from entering. She thought, *I'll just wait here at the entrance until Reece returns.* She couldn't imagine that he would be there very long. Waiting seemed the practical thing to do.

Laurel sat down on the curb, stretched out her legs and crossed them at the ankles. She put her arms out behind herself and leaned back on the grass, turning her face up to the sun. It felt wonderful shining down on her like that. A warm glow seemed to drift over her. She felt like she might even lie down and rest her eyes for a few minutes. She put her hands behind her head, leaned back and lay down on the grass behind the curb. She felt totally relaxed and at peace. Her mind seemed to open up with all kinds of thoughts. Her thinking became very clear. She lay there very quietly so that no one would pay any attention to her. She watched several people as they entered the park. Then it occurred to her that maybe there was another way into the park. If she were to walk up very close to someone who was going in, maybe she could slip in with them. But then, would she be able to get out? Unless, she could follow someone out the same way? Just then, Reece came walking out. She didn't need to worry herself about that anymore. He walked right past without even seeing her. "Reece!" she called out.

He turned and exclaimed, "Laurel, What are you doing here?"

"I came to see you," she said eagerly. "I was wondering why you left so early this morning."

He suddenly became very elusive, and said "You shouldn't have followed me here."

"Why?" she asked feeling hurt with his attitude.

"You just shouldn't have," he said rudely. "I have things I must do, and…" His words trailed off, and he started walking away. Laurel followed in disbelief.

"Why are you acting like this?"

"I can't get involved with you right now. I have a job to do and I can't...I just can't."

"You can't get involved with me? What was last night? Exactly what is that job you have to do? To see to it that I am made to feel better about this place! So I won't be agitated with everything around here! Is that it, huh, is it? I thought you loved me! I thought you loved me!" she pleaded. He wouldn't answer, but kept on walking away. She stood still, unable to move and let him go. She was sure, that she must be right about his job being to "take care of her," since he had not responded to her question, and he was very good at it because it had almost worked. She had felt complete just a few minutes before and now, she felt as if she had been thrown away. She dropped her head and looked down at the pavement. Tears streaming down her face. She walked back to the curb in front of the park gates and sat down. Covering her face with her hands, she cried openly. Reece hadn't gotten far, and he turned to see her one more time. He couldn't bear to see her so distraught. He ran back to her side and sat down beside her. She pulled away suddenly so hurt that she couldn't bear to have him touch her.

He tried to calm her by putting his arm around her, as he said, "Please forgive me, I didn't mean to hurt you. I do love you." Tears came into his eyes as he spoke, "I'm afraid."

"Afraid of what?" she asked suspiciously through her own tears.

"Afraid that I'll love you too much, and you'll leave me again. I don't know if I can stand that. While you were away, I thought you had left *The Keeping Place*, and I felt lost and alone. I've been happy here, but now without you here, when you go, everything will seem empty. You keep telling me that you want to leave."

"Of course I want to leave, and you should too. Come with me!"

"I can't. I can't leave this place."

"Why can't you leave?"

"I can't tell you that, but know that I truly love you," he said, and he kissed his fingers and placed them on her forehead. He rose to leave again, and this time he hurried away without looking back.

Laurel sat on the curb unable to grasp what had just happened.

She didn't know how to feel. The last few hours had been like a bungee jump between Heaven and Hell. The ups and downs were as wild as anything she had ever experienced. Maybe Reece was sincere and he really did love her, but he had left her without fully explaining himself. She didn't know what to do. She was stunned. The "Rosy Exposure" theory was having a hard time having any effect on her. Like a robot she started walking back toward her apartment.

When Laurel reached her apartment, she threw herself onto the bed and sobbed her heart out until there were no more tears left to cry. She had wanted to lie there on the bed and just die. Finally, she sat up on the bed and tried to think of what to do. A few minutes later there was a knock at the door. She tried to wipe her tear stained face with her shirt tail. She couldn't imagine who it could be, now when she just wanted to be left alone. She had thought Reece was her savior, and then the whole world fell apart, again. She opened the door, hoping it might be Reece, only to find the desk clerk standing there with a message in his hand. It was from Dr. Statten. She was to meet Charles in one hour at her hotel. He had apparently arranged the meeting with the children that she had requested. She would have to pull herself together. It wouldn't be wise to let him, or the children see her like this. Once again, she would be put to the test. She was a survivor!

# CHAPTER THIRTY

Kim awoke around 5:00 a.m. on the fateful morning. This was the day she would agree to remove the life support from Laurel. She had hardly slept at all, and was glad for the day to begin, to get it over.

James was preparing to take his patient off life support. He was examining her vital signs, and he noticed some rapid eye movement that he had not been aware of before. Also, her pulse rate seemed to be racing, and then it would return to normal. *Unusual,* he thought, *it worries me to see that pulse rate so erratic.* At one point in the examination he noticed a change in her brain waves, but it was only for an instant. He was monitoring her condition very closely. If this continued, he would suggest that they wait another few days for her to stabilize. That was the last thing he wanted to do after having waited so long for Kim to make this decision, but the safety of his patient was the most important thing.

James stood by the bed keeping his eyes on the monitors. Watching every movement. This certainly had been an unusual case. First, the patient being in such a terrible state when they brought her in, and then to see her fully recover from her physical injuries that under normal conditions would have taken the life of most people. The will to live had been very strong with this patient. Most people lose the will to live after sustaining such physical damage. But, this patient had faced death, and was fighting to live each day. Her strength was what had made him sure that he could bring her back. If only he could have convinced Kim to do this sooner.

Lately, James had seen some signs of deterioration that disturbed him. It was his feeling that this was probably the last chance this girl had for a normal life. Even though she appeared to be very strong, the physical body can only withstand so much stress. If she didn't wake up after they removed the support system, he felt she would surely whither and die. She had not yet assumed the fetal position, a sure sign of regression, but he felt certain that it was just a matter of time.

Through most of the time Laurel had been in the hospital, James had kept a low profile with Kim. After the first three or four months of seeing her every day, he had gotten to know her pretty well. But then, after realizing that she was not ready to work with him on this case, he only contacted her every couple of months to reiterate the need for removing the machines from Laurel. Why she was fighting this procedure was a mystery to him. He couldn't understand why she hadn't felt the urgency he had felt to remove Laurel from the life support system. *It only stands to reason that she would be better off without them,* he thought. *There is less stress on her body and mind when she can be in control of her own destiny.* The system and the medications were slowly, but surely destroying her physically. As far as he could see it was now or never.

James began to feel a closeness to Kim that he could only assume was because of the two people they had in common, Laurel and Reece. He had practically placed himself in an unattainable position to most people. Most of his friends had fallen away since the problems with Reece, but it was because of him, not them. He had several women interested in him, but he avoided them as often as he could. There were times when he had to attend a function where a date was important to his position at the hospital that he would seek one of them out, but he never found any of them to be interesting enough to spend any time with over an extended period of time. Kim was different…more interesting than most. She seemed to have a depth to her that he found intriguing, and she was by far, the most attractive woman he had ever seen. She seemed to get prettier each time he saw her, and he had a hard time keeping his mind entirely on his work when they were supposed to be discussing Laurel's condition. He thought he might like to get to know her better, but he wasn't quite sure how to approach the subject. He would bide his time, and see what happened in the future. Perhaps, if Laurel came out of the coma, Kim would see him in a different light. Although, that thinking had nothing to do with his decision to do this procedure. Laurel was his patient and his main concern for the time being, and if anything came of the relationship later, he would be happy to deal with it at that time, and not before.

# CHAPTER THIRTY-ONE

Charles arrived exactly on the hour he had arranged. Laurel was waiting in the lobby as she presumed she was expected to do since she was notified by the desk clerk that he was meeting her at the hotel. He hadn't specified exactly where they were to meet. Laurel thought it better to meet in the lobby than in her room. She had been staring out the front window of the hotel. Her thoughts were far away thinking of the events of the morning when she caught sight of Charles coming through the front door of the hotel. She turned toward him and tried to smile. He returned the smile, but he seemed a little agitated that she had come down to the lobby.

"There was no need for you to wait here in the lobby. I would have gladly picked you up at your door." He had hoped to spend a few minutes alone with her in her room. He wanted to talk to her about more personal things in quiet surroundings, but he would have to do that later.

"Oh, I'm sure you would have. I needed some air. I thought I would come down here and wait for you. Sometimes I get a little bored just sitting in my room," she said, trying to be pleasant for a change.

"Well, we'd better be on our way if we are going to get there on time. I told the administrator we would arrive by 3 o'clock." They walked out of the building and headed in a direction that Laurel had not expected to go. They walked around behind the hotel, and had walked only a short distance when they entered a building that looked like a subway tunnel. Laurel had almost forgotten her distress and was getting caught up in the adventure that she was about to embark upon.

She said almost with a question, "I was not aware that there was this kind of transportation available here."

"Yes, I'm sure you were not. The longer you are here, the more you'll find out about this world." The train pulled up and they got on.

"Don't you have to have a ticket?"

"Of course not. As you have seen before, we are provided with everything we need. It is just a short distance to the children's facility, but it would test you if you had to walk there." They rode the train for about 15 minutes and then it pulled into another station where they got off. The trip was through a tunnel above ground. There were windows at intervals where she could see glimpses of scenery.

"I wanted to get here a little early so you could see the grounds around the building before we see the children," Charles said. He acted excited, like a child himself. Laurel wondered why he would behave in such a manner until he said, "I lived here as a child, and also went to school here. My mother and father left me at an early age, and I was raised by a nanny. She was like a mother to me. It was a wonderful place to grow up. I was really glad when you said you wanted to come here." Laurel thought, this must not be like the orphanages she had known. In her estimation, being raised without your real parents wasn't at all a pleasant situation. She wondered if the "Rosy Exposure" had anything to do with his thinking this was such a grand place in which to live. She was going to observe everything carefully, and evaluate in her own mind whether or not this place was worthy of that kind of praise.

The grounds were as beautiful as Charles had said. She wouldn't have expected anything less since everything in this world…This place called *The Keeping Place* was beautiful. If she hadn't been so anxious to get back home to her own world, she might have actually enjoyed being here. Few places she had ever been before compared to the beauty around her while in this foreign world.

Charles led Laurel around the grounds showing her different places that he had enjoyed as a child. He began explaining more about his life.

"When a person, like me, is born here we live here until we reach adulthood and then take our place in the professional world. We acquire knowledge from birth and are groomed for the profession that best suits our abilities. We are kept separate from the sick children."

"What do you mean 'sick' children."

"The children who have come here through no fault of their own, and who are here for their bodies to heal. They are the ones you're here to see today. I think we should go in now. They will be expecting us." Laurel followed Charles as he ushered her through the front doors of the building. They were greeted by a very pleasant woman who was the director of the facility.

"Good afternoon, Dr. Statten," she said, as she reached out to shake his hand.

"Good afternoon," he replied. "This is Ms. Laurel Richards. Laurel, this is Mrs. Murdock, our Director. Mrs. Murdock, as I related to you earlier, Ms. Richards is eager to see the children."

"Well, we are very happy to allow you to see the children, Ms. Richards," she said, as she reached for her hand. Although, you must realize that there can be no physical contact between you and them. You see, it would be too traumatic for them. They are such delicate creatures. You can watch them through a viewing area."

*Creatures*, Laurel thought, *was a strange way to describe children.* The two of them were escorted down a hallway, and into a darkened room. Through the viewing glass she could see children playing in a room that looked like a classroom. The window was a one-way glass with a mirror on the side that faced the children so they couldn't see who was watching them. There were several age groups in this particular room.

"Are there other rooms with other children?"

"Oh, yes," the woman said. "There are many rooms with all ages of children. The children are in classes during the day, and then they are sent to dormitories for sleeping. Some have separate rooms, while others share a large dormitory. It depends on the severity of their specific needs. We have nannies who will take care of two to three children at a time, giving them individual care when needed. It is a very organized program." Laurel watched the children play, and interact with the teachers and other children. They seemed happy. She could see that the "Rosy Exposure" had a purpose here.

"What happens to them if they decide to stay?" Laurel asked with concern.

"These children don't have the same options that an adult has, Charles said. "When their physical body heals, they *must* go back, and we don't wait for someone to call them back. An interesting thing about children though," he added, "they are always called back. If for some reason their physical body cannot heal, they are sent on to Elysian Fields. They are not kept here." Laurel had been told about Elysian Fields before. She didn't need to have that explained. She felt extraordinarily sad after hearing that remark. Even though Heaven should be a good place to be, it seemed unfair that they would be taken before they had time to grow up.

After quietly watching the children for awhile, Laurel excused herself to go to the ladies room. Mrs. Murdock gave her instructions as to where she could find one. Charles and the woman remained in the viewing room. She found the restroom, freshened up, and started to return to the viewing room when she heard strange sounds coming from a room a few doors down. She walked closer and stood quietly next to the door for a moment, listening. It was hard to make out what the sounds were. She decided it wouldn't hurt to take a peak inside the room. The door was not locked, and it opened easily.

There in the room encased in plastic cylinders against the walls were small children. Some were sitting down playing with toys while others seemed to be trying to communicate with other children in adjacent cylinders. She walked closer, and wondered why they were in the cylinders. Then one little girl with beautiful blond curls looked up at her. Laurel threw her hands up and covered her mouth in utter disbelief. She tried to muffle the sounds of anguish that were trying to come out of her mouth. She couldn't move! Then, all the children turned their heads to look at Laurel. She started to scream without realizing where the sound was coming from. Suddenly she turned and ran from the room letting the door slam behind her.

Charles and Mrs. Murdock came running from the viewing room. A nurse in the hallway tried to stop her, but Laurel nearly knocked her over as she kept running, trying to find a way out of the building.

Charles ran after her and as he reached her he grabbed her by the arms and yelled at her, "What have you been doing? Where did you go?" he demanded. She had one hand over her mouth, and her eyes were frantic. Her whole body was shaking violently.

"Their faces!" she exclaimed. "They have no faces!"

"Quick!" Charles said to the nurse, "we're going to have to sedate her." He was afraid she was going into shock because now he realized where she had been. She was completely out of control of her emotions. The nurse ran to get the medication, and returned immediately with a hypodermic needle filled with the sedative. She jabbed it into Laurel's arm while Charles held her tightly. Laurel was so stunned that she couldn't have moved if she had wanted to. They quickly moved her into another room where Charles lifted her onto a bed. Her voice trailed off as she kept repeating, "Their faces.... their faces......In just a few minutes her twitching body gave way to the sedative and she slipped into a sleep that kept her completely oblivious to anything or anyone around her until they could decide what to do with her now. Now that she had seen the "Special Children."

# CHAPTER THIRTY-TWO

James had been watching his patient very closely. He had been anxious to remove the life support, but now he wasn't sure they should rush this procedure. After a year, a few more days wouldn't matter. All night, he had watched Laurel, checking every vital sign, and had noticed strange things happening. Her pulse rate had remained erratic. Sometimes, she would be perfectly normal and then, suddenly her pulse rate would soar. He was becoming worried. In the last few minutes her heart rate had almost jumped off the chart.

He yelled out, "My God! What's happening here?" He pushed the button for a nurse to come to his aid. He was wondering if there was something wrong with the equipment.

"There must be something wrong with these machines," he said to the nurse. She went immediately to the equipment and started checking everything. She was pushing buttons, checking tubes frantically.

"There doesn't seem to be anything wrong with the equipment, Doctor. Do you want me to sedate her?"

"Yes, I think we'd better give her a relaxant. Something to subdue her. We want her to come out of this coma, not throw herself into shock and die on us. I want her put under constant observation. I want an attendant here with her every minute for the next 24 hours."

James didn't want to postpone this procedure, especially since he had hounded Kim to make the decision. For the sake of the patient, he decided he should contact Kim and have her come down to the Care Center. He wanted to explain what was happening.

When the phone rang, Kim had been contemplating what she was going to do with the shop. She had been running it entirely by herself. Running the shop during the day, and doing the paperwork by night was such a hardship she wasn't sure she could continue. She had been thinking she should hire someone to take Laurel's place for awhile. She thought she could handle everything by herself, but

167

lately, she had come to the conclusion that she was beginning to suffer "burn out." Even if Laurel were to snap out of the coma, it would be a long time before she could return to the store. Kim had put money away for Laurel that she would have earned had she been in a position to work. The person she would hire would have to take over most of Laurel's responsibilities.

The ringing of the phone brought Kim out of her thoughts suddenly. "Good morning, this is the Treasure Shop," she said in a business-like manner.

"Good morning Kim," James said, as he got right to the point. "I'm afraid we may have to postpone our plans for today."

"What do you mean?"

"Well, I need you to come down to the center. We have to discuss the situation."

"Would you please get to the point! Quit being so vague!" Kim demanded. "I think I can handle just about any situation by now. What is it?"

"I think this is something you will have to see for yourself. If you wouldn't mind, I think you should get here as soon as possible."

"Is Laurel okay?"

"Please, just come down here as quickly as you can," he said and then, he hung up the phone. Kim was becoming more and more agitated with James's attitude along with being very concerned with the idea that something may be wrong with Laurel. She decided that the only thing to do was to close the shop. She posted a sign on the door saying the shop would be closed for the rest of the day, grabbed her coat and hailed a taxi.

When she arrived at the Care Center, she hurriedly paid the taxi driver and headed toward the building, nearly running. The weather had turned cold and snowy. She walked carefully trying not to slip on the icy sidewalk. James was waiting for her in the lobby. Without saying a word, James helped Kim with her coat, and folded it over his arm as he lead her down the corridor to the elevators.

As they waited for the elevator to arrive James began, "We've had a surprising turn of events since I last saw you. Everything was going according to our plans, until this morning. I've been watching her very carefully since early this morning, and I'm not sure what's going on. That's why I couldn't explain it over the telephone." The elevator door opened, and they walked in. Kim noticed that James looked worried as he pushed the button to the second floor. Kim felt a kind of weird apprehension, not knowing what to expect in the next few minutes.

Kim and James entered the room where Laurel lay, still comatose and connected to all kinds of tubes that extended back to machines that whirred endlessly. There was a nurse sitting at her bedside watching a monitor, as James had instructed. As they approached the bed James asked the nurse if there had been any changes in the last few minutes since he had left the room.

"The relaxant has apparently started to work," she said. "She has been very calm for the past few minutes."

"What has been going on?" Kim asked.

"I was monitoring her condition when I noticed a lot of rapid eye movement. Then, I checked her pulse, and it was way too fast. We went through a series of tests, and found her heart beat to be erratic, as well. At that point, I wasn't sure we should go any farther with this procedure, at least until we can decide if it's safe. I am anxious to remove the machines, but not until we know for sure that she is ready. Her safety is what we are most concerned with." Kim felt drained. The anticipation of removing the tubes, and then this sudden change was another stressful situation that she had hoped she would not have to deal with. She sat down in the chair beside the bed and looked out the window. It has started to snow and a gloomy feeling engulfed her. James walked around the bed and put his hand on her shoulder.

"I know how hard this must be for you, but this is just a temporary setback. We'll watch her for the next few days, and then we can re-schedule the removal. And, if she stabilizes sooner, I'll contact you. Right now she is calm because of the sedative. We don't want to rush into this." Kim stood up and turned toward James.

"I hardly think a year is rushing into anything, but I do understand what you are saying." It was as if they had switched roles.

Surprisingly, since she was the one who originally didn't want to go through with this procedure, she was now the one who thought it should go forward without delay. She felt like this was just another thing to keep her from getting back to any kind of normal life. The life she had a year ago.

James could see that Kim wasn't taking this delay very well. He put his hands on her shoulders and looked into her eyes and said, "It'll be okay." This was all she needed to bring forth the tears that she had been trying to hold back. He drew her close to him and he put his arms around her holding her tightly as her body shook with sadness. During their time together, he had grown very fond of her, and hated to see her going through, yet another setback. Under other circumstances, he might have thought of her in a romantic way, but right now he had too much on his mind to let those kinds of emotions enter into this situation. His own life was a mess, with Reece in this same Center, and lately, his mother's failing health along with all of his patients needing a bedside manner that he had to pull up from the depths of his very soul. But, he was hanging on, and giving care wherever it was needed most. It was needed here today. He would come through again. Strong as usual. He wondered if there would ever come a time when he could just let down and be himself. But, not today.

IN *THE KEEPING PLACE:*

Charles sat across from Laurel waiting for her to come out of the tranquilized state which he and the nurse had induced. He hadn't wanted her to be out very long. He just wanted her to be in control of her emotions. He knew what she had seen would be shocking to someone, like her, from another world, but he hadn't intended for this visit to be a traumatic thing. And, it wouldn't have been had she stayed where she was supposed to be. He admonished himself silently by saying to himself that he should have watched her more closely, but he hadn't even suspected she would go wandering around. But, now that she had, he was going to have to explain what she had seen. She was his responsibility.

Charles wondered how he would explain something that in his own world seemed so simple and normal, yet in her world would seem so bizarre. Laurel started to move, and Charles was sure she was about to awaken. He reached over and took her hand in his and looked down at it with admiration as he gently massaged it. When she spoke, he looked up abruptly, and smiled at her thinking a friendly attitude might make it easier for her to remain calm. She tried to pull her hand away from his as she asked him what had just happened.

"I know you're upset," he started and she interrupted him.

As soon as she was able to regain her composure she said, "Upset? I don't think you know the meaning of upset, or how upset I really am!"

"I know more about you than you may think."

She began again with tears in her eyes and her voice shaking, "Just when I start to think everything is almost normal here, something else happens to bring me back to reality. I think this place is some kind of house of horrors. I saw those poor children, those poor horrible children!"

"Now, wait a minute. Those children are just fine, there is nothing horrible about them." he said in exasperation. "Laurel, there are many things that you don't know anything about in this world. Things that you would never have been exposed to if you had just stayed within your realm like most people."

"That's exactly what concerns me about this place. You want me, and everyone else, to stay in this little *realm,* or prison to be more precise. You want me to be happy with everything around me without questioning anything. Isn't that a little communistic?"

"I don't know what you mean by communistic. We don't have a bureaucratic system here like you have in your world." Charles sighed, and continued, "I'm going to try to tell you whatever you may need to know or think you need to know. We don't want to have anymore of these unexpected catastrophes. Each time I feel like we have given you what you need, and then you surprise me with some off the wall thing that should never have happened. First, if you can remember, I told you before that you are in a transcendental holding area called *The Keeping Place*. It's a holding place for lots and lots of people, not just for you. It's a place for children too. Our only purpose for being who, and what *we are* is to keep you and them happy. Therefore, we would never...and I repeat.... never do anything to harm you, or anyone else. Is that clear?" he demanded.

She was not startled at his behavior this time. She had seen it before, and she answered hesitantly wondering what to expect next, "Ye...yes." Her widened eyes were glued on him as she listened intently.

"I have a responsibility to take care of you. All of the people who were born here have that responsibility. We even have to protect you from yourself, and with you, this has been a tremendous task. You are such a small part of this place, and yet you seem to think this whole world pivots around you. You are important to us, of course, but we have other people to take care of too, and you make that extremely difficult. Because of the problems you keep causing we have spent more time with you than we have with three-fourths of the other people here. We answer to a higher power than you could ever imagine. If we do something wrong, or we don't do our jobs efficiently, we are taken away. Everything we have done for you so far has been for your well being."

Charles started his explanation of what she had seen. "What you saw today wasn't something you should have seen, and since I am responsible for you, I feel I must try to explain. Those children are here for a very virtuous reason. They have been born to people who have been here for quite awhile. Two people have fallen in love, and consummated their relationships. If a child is born to a couple from a union such as this and then, they are unexpectedly called back through *The Veil*, they have no choice but to leave that child here. Children like that cannot pass through *The Veil*. They are not strong enough to withstand the force. Then, those children will simply wait here until a new soul comes for them."

"How does a soul come for them?"

"When a baby from your world dies suddenly, for whatever reason, for a fleeting moment as the soul prepares to leave the body,

172

that body slips into a coma and the soul comes here. At that time, one of those children that *you* saw will become whole by taking on that soul. That soul will then continue on with a full life. They will have a chance to grow up, have families and live a life much the same as children would in your world. This is how they gain moral values and a testimony of life that was taken from them at the time of their removal from your world. They need this life experience so they can make the choices all of us have to make. Then, a time will come when they must decide whether they want to stay here, or move on to Elysian Fields where their life will continue, but at a different spiritual level. Death as you know it to be, is not a sad thing in our world. Here it's called a re-birth. It's simply another level of life."

"But, they have no faces!" Laurel exclaimed.

"Only to you they have no faces. To us they are just as normal as any other child. You are only supposed to see what you need to see while you're here. You were not supposed to see them."

If I were to look at one of them, I would see a beautiful child that will, someday, belong to a beautiful soul. Right now they live in a holographic world while they wait for that spirit to come for them."

"If I were to look at them again, now, would I see faces?"

"No, only those who have received their souls would have faces. That's why we do not allow you, or anyone else to see them. Even if we prepared you to see them it would still be a shock to someone of your world. It is the natural course of lives within this realm, and totally normal. The reason they are here in the first place is *because* of your own world, and with the love of The Creator they will someday become whole. It is truly a beautiful thing. However, I can assure you that you will not be seeing them again. It's too traumatic for them to see you. Your screaming episode has upset them terribly by disrupting the holograms they were involved with, and it will take awhile to settle them down. The nurses are busy reassuring them now, and hopefully, they will soon be back to normal. Most of these children are very resilient. More so than the children from the viewing room, who are very fragile."

"What happens to a child who is 5 or 6, if their parents leave? Is it the same as when a baby is left?"

"No, they have already experienced life with their parents, and their personalities have already been developed. They will continue on with their lives here as they are. Their souls have already been secured."

"Those children, the ones I saw in the viewing room through the glass…what happens to them?" Laurel asked.

"The children in the viewing rooms are the ones who linger in a coma. They still have a chance of going back to your world, if their bodies heal properly. It is our responsibility to see to it that they are well taken care of until they have that opportunity," he said. "And, as I said before, children are always called back by their parents and friends. But, not all of them will be able to go back. If their bodies don't…or *can't* heal, they will not be returning to your world. It's sad for the people they have left behind, but for them personally, they will move on to Elysian Fields where they will live out the rest of their lives progressing through a series of life's lessons that The Creator has planned for them, they will become angels. Laurel was so moved by this information that she felt she must apologize for her behavior. It did appear that these children were being cared for with love and concern.

"I'm sorry," she said, hanging her head down. "I'm sorry I caused so much trouble. I was just curious when I heard the sounds coming from the room. I had no idea I would encounter such a place, and I wasn't looking for anything. I wasn't trying to hurt anyone." She was feeling a little bit like a fool, but she continued, "I don't think you can ever imagine how horrible it was for me to see them? I've never seen anything like that before in my entire life. I keep seeing images of those children with no faces. I hope I will be able to forget what I saw."

"I am sure you will, with time…we will see to it."

"Can we leave this place now?"

"Of course we can. I think you would feel better if we left. Stay here while I check with the nurses about the children, and I will be right back." As he left the room Laurel slipped off the bed and walked over to the window to gaze out over the facility grounds. She stood there for a moment and then she slowly walked over to the door. It seemed like it was taking forever for Charles to return. She slowly turned the knob…the door was locked! She could actually understand why they locked her in this room this time, but it still angered her. She felt she had learned her lesson. She folded her arms and stomped across the room to the window. As she stood looking through the glass, she saw Charles across the way talking to a nurse. They appeared to be in deep conversation. Laurel just stood there watching intently.

Laurel didn't want to be here anymore, and she wished he would hurry back. She was very tired after the events of the day, and she wanted to go back to her apartment. It seemed that lately she was tired all the time, and she cried at the drop of a hat. It was so unlike her usual self. But, of course, she hadn't seemed herself since she had been in this world. There wasn't anything she could do to change her situation. She decided to lie down on the bed until he returned, and with the quietness of the room she fell asleep within a few minutes.

# CHAPTER THIRTY-THREE

James had been at the Care Center all day. He hadn't wanted to leave until he was sure Laurel was stabilized. They had been watching her closely for the past 24 hours. He had spent the last hour just sitting by her bed watching the machines that monitored her vital signs. They appeared to be coming back to normal. Or at least, as normal as a coma patient can be. He looked down at her face, and he thought, *I wonder what she was like before this happened.* He tried to imagine what her personality might have been like. Then his mind switched back to a professional level and he moved closer to the machines to take a closer look at the gauges. He thought that if she remained stabilized, as she was now, they could probably remove the life support system tomorrow. Or perhaps, even this evening. He had asked Kim to be ready at a moments notice. He would keep his fingers crossed.

James sat back down in the chair by the bed, and closed his eyes for a moment. His thoughts went back to Reece in the room just down the hall. *How similar these two cases were, Reece and Laurel,* he thought. Of course, the reasons for their being in comas were completely different. Reece's having been self induced, and Laurel's having been by accident. But, the coma itself was what he was relating to.

Reece had been in his coma for more than two years, actually it was almost three years now. He had been in a coma for almost two years when Laurel came into the hospital. The time seemed like it had flown by since they had moved Laurel to the Care Center. James spent a lot of time here in this facility across from the hospital. He hadn't minded that time, though. Sometimes, it made him reflect on his life with his brother before all this happened. For many years there were happy times. It was only those last few months before he overdosed that were so stressful, when Reece was out of control.

The similarities James was thinking about were that both of these people were young when this happened to them. They both had been in a coma much longer than the average patient, and he was amazed at how well their physical bodies had responded to the condition they were in. Had either of them been older, they probably would not have lived this long. The trauma alone should have killed Laurel, under normal conditions. And then Reece, being wasted on drugs, was in terrible condition when this happened to him.

*There must be some reason they have both survived for this long,* James thought. Whatever it was, he hadn't a clue. As you look down into their faces, they seem to be in a peaceful sleep. Except for the rapid eye movement, and the changes that he had observed during the past couple of days with Laurel, there seemed to be no differences in either of the cases. They seemed to be progressing, if you can call it progressing, actually, they were just maintaining at the same rate. Very little deterioration at this time, although he had seen signs of slight differences in both patients. He was worried that they both might take a turn for the worse physically. At this point in time, he had little hope of ever seeing his brother regain consciousness again. However, he felt there was still hope for Laurel.

James was brought back to reality when the nurse walked in to relieve him for a few minutes.

"Wouldn't you like to stretch your legs…maybe take a little walk?" the nurse asked. "I'll watch her for awhile, and you can take a little break." He decided he probably should take a break for awhile.

"A cup of coffee would probably taste pretty good right now," he said with a half smile. It was all he could do to smile at all with all the stress of the last few hours.

"Thank you, I'll be back in about half an hour," he said, as he walked over to the door. "You page me if there are any changes, Okay?"

"You know I will, Doctor," the nurse said. "You just go and get your coffee, and relax for a few minutes. Everything will be okay here for awhile." He knew it was going to be a long night. He thought he would stop in to see Reece on his way back to Laurel's room after this break. He wanted to make sure everything was alright with him. He wondered how long this was going to go on, how long Reece would actually live like this, if you can call this living. His heart was heavy wondering if maybe it would be better if Reece died. And then, he would feel guilty for even having had those thoughts.

After having monitored Laurel most of the day James had his coffee and then rested for awhile in the doctor's lounge. It was still early evening, and after another examination of Laurel he decided that she appeared to be stable enough to begin the procedure this evening so, he called Kim to return to the Care Center. She had returned reluctantly thinking they probably should have waited until the next day, but she assumed the doctor knew what he was doing. She had been very impressed with James Martin, and was sure he would do the right thing. She walked into the Center, and took the stairs to Laurel's room on the second floor. James greeted her and asked her to stay by Laurel's bedside while they were turning off the machines. James told Kim that she might want to say a little prayer.

He said, "It couldn't hurt."

Kim had never been very religious, and didn't belong to an organized church, but she did believe there was a God and she did her best to think up a prayer. James and a nurse turned off several switches and another nurse removed the tubes from Laurel's wrists, nose and throat. They left the catheter in, in case there was a sudden surge of bodily fluids. The nurse first administered a shot of liquid Magnesium, waited a few minutes and then gave her a shot of Adrenalin.

"Now, all we can do is pray and hope for the best," James said.

As she sat by the bed, Kim looked at her friend, picked up her limp hand in hers and quietly said, "Laurel, please come back!"

James looked into Laurel's eyes with a light pulling her eyelids up as he examined her thoroughly. He saw no immediate changes. He could see no apparent reason for her to not come out of the coma. He believed her to be totally healthy. Kim slumped back in her chair, still holding Laurel's hand and covered her eyes with her other hand. She was feeling a terrible disappointment. James was feeling that same disappointment, only more severely since he felt responsible for the failure, if it were, indeed, a failure. He walked around and leaned on the edge of the bed by Kim, and folded his arms.

"I just don't know what to think, Kim. I was almost certain that this would bring her out of the coma. Maybe, if we give it a little time she will respond."

# CHAPTER THIRTY-FOUR

Laurel awoke suddenly. It seemed that she was always coming out of some kind of stupor. She looked around and realized that she was back in her apartment on her own bed. She wondered how this had happened. The last thing she remembered was falling asleep in the Children's Care Center after she had seen those strange children.

She felt dizzy, and she thought she had heard voices, but then assumed it must have been Charles, as he said, "Hello!" Laurel had a puzzled look on her face. "You're probably wondering what I'm doing here, aren't you?"

"Yes, I was thinking that, and how did I get here?" she asked as she sat up on the edge of the bed holding her head with both hands. She could feel her pulse beating in her head. "We were with the children and now, we're here? What's going on?"

"You were asleep when I returned to the examining room. I had you transported here. I thought you would be more comfortable here in your own surroundings. Besides, I have wanted to talk to you about something."

Very sarcastically Laurel said, "What could you possibly want to talk to me about here that you couldn't have talked to me about there?" She assumed that he wanted to talk to her about what had happened before with the children. She was totally surprised, and shocked when he started talking about his personal feelings for her.

"I have become very fond of you with the time we've spent together," he said, as he sat down on the side of the bed next to Laurel. He reached out and took Laurel's hand in his. She gently pulled it away feeling very uneasy about this conversation, not knowing where it was going to lead. She was beginning to feel extremely uncomfortable.

He continued being careful not to alarm her, "I don't mean to upset you in any way, but I was thinking that if you remain here, perhaps we could spend some time together other than on a professional level." Laurel wasn't sure if she even liked Charles. He had been less than nice the last few times she had been with him. They had a doctor/patient relationship, and that was as far as she wanted it to go.

"I'm not sure I fully understand your meaning, Dr. Statten," she said, trying to avoid the implications of his conversation.

Charles knew immediately, he had overstepped his bounds when she called him by his professional name, but he continued, "I know this must seem a little sudden. It's just that...I really like you and I would like to get to know you, more like a friend rather than a doctor/ patient association. There are lots of things I would like to show you here that I'm sure you would enjoy, and we could get to know each other better." Laurel got up from the bed, feeling like it was not wise to be sitting there with him in the room while he was acting this way. Although, she didn't really think she had anything to be afraid of.

"Are you saying that you want me to stay here?" she asked as she slowly walked across the room.

"Not exactly," he said. "I'm only saying that if you *should* decide you wanted to stay...I'll be here for you, to help you out, if you need anything...anything at all." He was actually being more vague than he wanted to be, but he didn't want to scare her away. Laurel thinking that she didn't know how to get out of this conversation thought it might be better to lead him on, rather than tell him outright how she felt. She had absolutely no feelings for this man, either romantically or otherwise. She wasn't even sure she wanted him for a friend. He had done nothing but confuse her since she had been here, and she wasn't sure she could trust him.

"I'm sure there are many things I would enjoy seeing, as you have said, but right now, I think you should leave," she said smiling, not wanting to upset him as she reached out her hand to say good-bye. Charles took her hand, and smiled slightly. He realized that he had made a mistake, and that she didn't have any of the same feelings he had for her. That was something he would have to deal with. He only hoped that he had not ruined their friendship. She had no idea of the depth of his feelings for her, and she considered him more of a threat than a friend. He would never have hurt her or anyone else for that matter, even though she wasn't aware of that quality in him. It was beyond anything in his reasoning to hurt anyone. He was genuinely a good person, and the good would come through as soon as he had time to think this out.

Charles had been very confused with his feelings lately. He was very much aware of the attraction he had for Laurel, and it was very disturbing. He had tried throughout is life to remove himself from having any feelings for the Spanners. He knew what he was feeling wasn't right. He had to make some changes, and needed to do some soul searching. He needed to make things right. It was not his position to put pressure on anyone who might be in transition, as Laurel was at this time. His position had placed him above such petty things, and he knew better than to interfere with a Spanner's life choices. Laurel had been trying to make a decision that would affect the rest of her life, and he wasn't helping matters with his flirtatious behavior. He decided that if Laurel wanted to go back to her own world, he would do everything in his power to help her.

Charles had found himself falling in love with Laurel, and he knew that unless she decided to stay, by her own volition, he had no right to interfere with her decisions. Whether those decisions included him, or Reece were only to be made by Laurel in her own time. His feelings about Reece also had to change. Maybe, that would be the place to start making things right. He would talk to Reece, and hoped it wasn't too late to rectify his actions. In his world, *The Keeping Place,* Charles had already made the right decisions to put him in good stead with his Superiors. Had Charles continued in the direction he was going, there would have been consequences to suffer.

Laurel felt immediately relieved to have Charles gone. She quickly changed from the jeans and sweater she was wearing into a blue silk dress and sandals, checked her makeup and hair, waited a few minutes to make sure he had left the building, and she headed out to look for Reece. She wanted to talk to him right away about Charles' behavior. It had been very troubling to her. She just needed someone to talk to. She was also curious about being "transported" from one place to another. She wondered if that were an option here, to use as a means to reach a destination. If it were, she wanted to know more about it. It was another unusual and curious thing about this place. She would ask Reece about it if she could find him.

As soon as Laurel stepped out of the building she began to feel better. "Rosy Exposure" was always there, and she could count on it to take immediate effect and make her feel better. When she thought about it, it wasn't so bad. She wondered how it would be to live your whole life in a place where you always felt good, things always turn out right, and everything was beautiful and serene. She decided right then that if she had to stay, maybe it would be alright. But, she would still try to go home if at all possible.

Reece spent a lot of time at the park. That was where Laurel would look for him first. She saw him sitting on a bench outside of the park almost as if he had been waiting for her. She was beginning to wonder if he really did have a medical practice at all. He seemed to have a lot of free time. She walked over and sat down beside him on the bench. They didn't say anything at all for a long few seconds.

Then, Reece said, "I'm glad you came back. I thought you might so I waited here for you."

It was a little awkward at first, but she smiled, and trying to ease into a conversation asked, "Do you really work someplace? You seem to be able to come and go as you please. Can you transport yourself to anywhere you want? Charles just had me transported to my apartment. I'm very curious about that."

"I can do whatever, or go anywhere I want here. Transporting does play an important part of our lives here."

"How does it work?"

"It's just a simple mind over matter thing. If you want to go somewhere, you just think seriously about it, and you *will* yourself to go there. It works very well. And, more importantly, any time you need me I will be available for you," he said. She was touched with his sincerity, and completely astonished with that idea of transportation. She leaned over to rest her head on his shoulder for a moment before she started to tell him what she had just experienced.

"Have you seen the children at the Care Center here?"

"Yes, I have," he said with a questioning look at her. "What about them?"

"Well, Charles took me to see them today. I saw all of them. Even the ones without faces." Reece had a puzzled look on his face when she said that.

"What do you mean, no faces?" he asked incredulously. He was starting to worry about her. He knew she had been upset lately, but this was very strange. *This seemed a strange thing for her to be saying,* he thought. Those children hadn't seemed strange to him because he had seen the children after he had become a Stayer, and not before. What he saw was totally normal. He didn't have any idea what she was talking about.

"You haven't seen them? You really haven't seen them, have you?"

"I don't know what you are talking about. All of the children I saw had faces. Are you sure you're alright?"

Laurel thought for a moment then she said, "There must be things going on here that only Charles, and a few others know about, and apparently you have not been told. I can't believe you didn't know," she said. "I saw them and I was very upset, and I'm still upset. And then, Charles transported me back to my apartment, but while we were there he became very friendly to me. It made me feel uncomfortable."

"You've had quite a day, haven't you?" he said, trying not to be condescending. "I really don't think there's anything wrong with someone being friendly, is there?"

"Well, I think it was more than just friendship he was offering." she said. Reece could see he needed to handle this situation a little bit differently. He needed to convince her that there were more important issues that needed to be tended to. He didn't believe she was being rational enough to know just what she actually did see. *Children without faces,* he thought, *How ridiculous.* He had never heard of such a thing, but he'd had no involvement with children since he had been here. *Perhaps, there is more to this story than I know*, he thought. *I'll check into it, but not now. I'm sure there is a logical reason for whatever Charles is doing.*

Reece reached out and put his arms around Laurel, and kissed her tenderly on the forehead. She looked up at him with surprise, and the calming effect it had on her made her melt in his arms as his lips moved down to hers.

He kissed her again and said, "I don't want you to worry about that right now. I want you to spend the rest of the time you have here with me." That was just what she had been waiting to hear. She thought about what he said, *"The rest of the time you have here,"* and *she wondered how much time that would be.* They sat for awhile in the warm sun embracing each other, and letting the world go on around them. It seemed that all the bad things that had happened were slowly slipping away.

# CHAPTER THIRTY-FIVE

Laurel was thinking how nice it was to have this overwhelming feeling of love all around her. She felt drenched in it, almost lost in the feeling when she suddenly came to her senses realizing that she had almost let herself believe that she might actually be happy here. *What must she be thinking*, she thought. Something odd that kept happening was that every once in awhile she would see flashing lights, and she wondered where they were coming from? That would bring her back to reality for a moment, but then it was too peaceful here with Reece to let that spoil her time with him. She looked into Reece's eyes and felt drawn deep down inside them to a heart that beckoned her to stay forever. *She must be strong*, she thought.

She said, "Reece, have you ever thought you might like to change your mind, and go back home?"

"No, I've told you before, I love it here. I have never been this happy anywhere else. There is something here that makes life worth living for me. Each day when I wake up I feel joy, and I think you could too."

"Yes, I understand what you are talking about. I've felt it too. I call it 'Rosy Exposure'," she said, laughing timidly.

"Laugh if you will, but it means a lot to me to feel this way. I never felt this way in our world. I couldn't get past the constant expectation to be perfect. I was always trying to solve problems, until it overwhelmed me, and I lost control of everything, my whole life was ruined by my own stupidity. Now, I'm living an adventure, and I'm having the time of my life, enjoying every minute of it." While she sat next to Reece, Laurel felt joy too.

"Isn't there more to life than to feel total happiness," she asked absently as if talking to herself. "Or is *that* what life is really all about." She had once heard someone say, 'life is an adventure to be lived, not a problem to be solved'. *Could this be what they meant? Could she feel real happiness here living a mystery of life, and never miss her own world, or would she eventually tire of this feeling of bliss, and find this life shallow and empty.* She would never know unless she went back and then, it would be too late, or would it? But, she had to try. It wouldn't be fair to Reece not to be sure of herself. On the other hand, would it be fair to her friends on the other side of *The Veil* if she didn't try to go back. She was confused. She started to question what *would* be fair for herself. Maybe, it was time to think about herself. What would be best for her with, or without Reece? She couldn't bear to loose Reece now.

She asked, trying to delve into his mind to find the real reason he wouldn't go back.

"Do you ever feel like you're being a coward staying here where there's no stress, no adverse feelings, no challenges?"

"No, I don't. I've felt more like a person here than ever before. The work I do here is important. I'm helping people everyday. It makes me feel like I'm re-paying society for the messes I've caused, and as for challenges, everyday is a challenge, because of the differences I encounter here. I'm happy, and no matter what anyone else says or does, that will not change for me. As long as I live an exemplary life here I am guaranteed of that happiness for an eternity." Only too aware that he should not be trying to persuade her either way, he said quietly, "This could be your life too."

"If life here is what I've seen so far, I'm not impressed."

"You haven't seen anything, Laurel. There is so much to see here that you haven't been allowed to see. There are wonderful people here, and wonderful places to see. It's a whole new world. You've only seen what you needed to see to make your healing complete." He was becoming very animated with hand gestures, "It's like Disneyland, Sea world, Barnum & Bailey's Circus…and the oceans, and mountains…any fantasy that you can imagine is here to be explored. I can't even describe the wonders of this place to you."

"Is this really the truth?" she asked unbelievingly.

"Absolutely, I would never lie to you. There is one thing I can promise you," he said in a more serious mood.

"And what is that?" she asked with a half smile.

"If you should decide to stay, I can promise you that I will love you forever," he said. "But, it's not fair for me to try to keep you here. I won't try to dissuade you anymore. As much as it hurts me to let you go, I must."

"Come with me!" Laurel pleaded. "You could change your mind and return with me!"

"No, I can't! We've had this conversation before, and you know I can't," he said, and he became very somber. "You don't know what I did in our world."

"Then, tell me about it!" she demanded.

"Alright," he relented. "I…I was into drugs heavily, and…I even stole drugs from the hospital where I worked. If I were to go back I would be prosecuted, and incarcerated for a long time. Maybe, for the rest of my life."

She tried to reassure him, "It's not a life sentence for drug possession. You would probably be out in a few years."

"Yeah, and then what? I was never cured of the addiction, and besides that, there's more," he paused. "I…I…killed a man!" He stopped suddenly because of the shock he saw on Laurel's face. "It was an accident. He got in the way when I was taking the drugs out of the cabinet in the hospital. I shoved him and he fell, he hit his head on the corner of a table." Reece started to cry and buried his head in his hands. "I never meant to hurt anyone," he said through tears. "He was my friend. He was just trying to stop me from ruining my life." Laurel reached out her hand to stroke his head, but then, pulled it back. She was crying too, but couldn't bring herself to touch him.

"So you see, Laurel," he cried as he looked into her eyes, "why I can *never* go back?" Laurel was numb. She turned and couldn't face him for a moment. She had no words to describe her feelings. She didn't say a word, she couldn't. The words just wouldn't come.

Reece suddenly stood up and said, "I have to go now. I can see I've upset you, and you're the last person in this world I would ever want to hurt," and he hurried away. Laurel still couldn't move or think. She sat there for a few minutes looking up into the cloudless sky. Then she saw what she thought were flashing lights, and her head hurt as she tried to understand what had occurred when she caught a glimpse of Reece standing in front of her, as if he had never left.

He had returned, and he said, "Look! There is one thing I can do for you. I've messed up everything else I've ever tried to do, but maybe I can make it right by trying to help you go back. If you're sure that this is really what you want? I love you Laurel, and it hurts me more than you will ever know to let you go, but I'll do this for you."

"No," she said through her tears. "I'm not sure that's what I want to do now. I love you too. I'm not sure I can go back now, and forget about you. I'm not sure I want to."

"You have to try," he said reassuringly. "Otherwise, you'll never be sure you made the right choice."

"Is there any way I can come back if I decide I have made the wrong decision?" she asked anxiously.

"Yes, there is, but it's risky. If you only stay there a short period of time you can *will* yourself back here, if you try hard enough. But, you can't stay long. If you stay too long it will be too late, and you would never be able to return. I want you to know that if you should decide to come back, I'll be waiting for you with all the love you could ever imagine. Please try to remember me!"

"I will, I will. I could never forget you, I love you Reece," she said. Reece pulled her close to him and kissed her with a passion she could never forget.

He became very serious, as he said, "There is something you need to know. Something that almost no one but the Guardians know. Charles told me to tell you this. You know, he's really a good guy, maybe a little misguided, and confused, but he's alright. He's sorry he upset you today."

"Charles is trying to help me?"

"Yes, it was always his intention to help you. You just couldn't see it because of your anger about being here. This is his way of letting you know that he was always sincere in his attempts to make it easier for you to be here. Anyway, he said it is very important for you to understand what I am about to tell you. Listen carefully! There is a time element involved. Have you ever looked at a clock and noticed that the time is exactly 2:22, 3:33 or any time that has all the same three or four digits?"

He didn't wait for an answer, and Laurel had a confused look on her face as he continued, "Whether you have, or not doesn't matter. Just listen. The point is, when time is at *that* place, that is the time when a person is most vulnerable. That's when, if you have been traumatized, you will slip into a coma. Some people are more susceptible than others. Most people have no idea that time has anything to do with it, but believe me, that is the most important factor involved."

"You mean that when I was in the car accident, the time factor was what put me here?" she asked.

"Yes, it's true. Time is essential to our very being. At the very second you were in trauma, time was moving into a precise position to allow you to slip into *The Veil*. It's almost like a tunnel that you have fallen through."

"Then, my being here was really a twist of fate?"

"No, not at all. That isn't what I was trying to convey to you. You were meant to be here. Things happen for a reason in this universe. I'm explaining this to you so you'll understand the importance of what I am about to say. If you should decide to return, watch the time. You can only return at a precise time. Do you understand me?" he asked her as he took hold of her shoulders and looked directly into her eyes.

She nodded, unable to say a word, and then he said, "Its time to go. Are you ready?"

She thought long and hard for a few seconds and asked with resolve, "Alright, what do I have to do?"

"*The Veil* that you must pass through is here in the park," he said. "That is why you were never allowed to enter before." Now, Laurel understood the barrier that had kept her out. She had always thought that she would have to return to the place where she had entered this world.

*No wonder it hadn't worked before when I tried to leave by going down the highway,* she thought. *That was only an entrance, and this place in the park is only an exit.*

"The only way you can get into the park is to stand as close to me as you can. Put your arms around me and we will walk through the entrance together, as one."

With that plan, they walked through the entrance without a problem to a place that looked like a whirling wind tunnel, and Laurel said, "I thought I would have to be called back to the other side. How can this work?"

"You have been called back. The time has come." Now, she understood why Charles had said she would not be able to leave by herself. Someone would have to show her the way, and apparently Reece was the one. The wind was blowing through her hair as she stood there holding onto Reece tightly. She wasn't sure she understood what was happening, what her feelings really were. She had waited such a long time for this, and now she wasn't sure if she really wanted to leave. Especially without Reece, the only man she had ever loved. Could she leave him? Her heart was aching as she was being pulled away. She reached out to him.

"Please come with me," she pleaded.

"You know I can't my love," he said as he kissed her hand, and let it fall away. She could see the tears in his eyes as she slowly slipped into *The Veil*.

Laurel remembered saying one last word, "Wait!" But, it was too late. She was being pulled through a long whirling hole. She thought she should be afraid, but the fear didn't come. She was very calm while she watched everything going by her as if it were in slow motion. People...men...women...children...were whooshing past her. She had seen no one else at the opening of *The Veil* when she entered, and now there were hundreds of people passing her, floating. They appeared to be oblivious to anything around them, like they were in a trance. Like angels. She began to wonder if she had died, and this was the passage to heaven. Then, as if nothing had happened at all, she found herself lying in a hospital bed with Kim sitting beside her holding her hand. She had come home.

# CHAPTER THIRTY-SIX

Kim and James were discussing what to do next when suddenly, Laurel's eyes opened. Neither of them saw what was happening. They were too involved with their own grief to notice. Kim still had hold of Laurel's hand when she felt a pressure, a tightening, like a squeeze. Kim looked back at Laurel suddenly, and seeing her eyes open she started to cry and laugh at the same time. She had waited so long for this moment, and yet, she couldn't believe it was actually happening. Laurel was awake...and alive...and real once again.

Kim could hardly contain her joy at seeing Laurel wake up. She held her hand to her mouth, trying to hold onto her emotions. Trying to be calm. "Laurel, you're awake!" was all she could say half crying, half laughing. Laurel tried to speak, but no words would come. Until, she uttered, "I'm so tir...ed. I need to sleeeeep," and she closed her eyes and drifted into a peaceful sleep. Kim stood up and backed away from the bed, as James took out his stethoscope and started examining Laurel. Kim was afraid she had gone back into the coma, but James assured her that Laurel was only sleeping.

"She seems to be fine," James said delightedly. "Her breathing is normal. Her pulse was normal. I am very pleased to see this kind of recovery. If you would like to leave for awhile, and come back later...I'm sure the nurses will be able to watch over her until you return."

"I can't leave her now, I've waited too long."

Just then, a nurse hurried in and whispered something to Dr. Martin.

"It's your brother, Doctor," she said. He immediately became alarmed and excused himself from the room. The nurse had summoned him to Reece's room. Kim had decided to stay by Laurel's side in case she woke up. She wanted to be there. James had previously moved Reece onto the same floor as Laurel's room because of the time he had to spend with each of them. The move had made it easier to see both patients. The room was just two doors away. He hurried down the hall as the nurse led the way.

"There is something going on with him, Doctor, his vital signs are very erratic," she said, acting very nervous. As James reached the side of his brother's bed, he could see what she meant. He was sweating profusely, and seemed to be in some kind of pain or discomfort. After examining him, James found that Reece's heart rate was becoming irregular, and his breathing was becoming labored. James was worried. After having such a recovery with his other patient this evening, to lose Reece now would be devastating.

James had thought if such a recovery were possible with her, maybe there was still hope for Reece. But, now he was unsure what was going to happen. James had Reece placed on oxygen, which was in no way putting him back on life support. It would simply make it easier for him to breath. He did all he could to make Reece comfortable, but it was to no avail. Reece had gone into Acute Renal failure, and there was nothing they could do to save him. It had happened too fast. In a few minutes his heart stopped beating and his life was over. James tried everything to resuscitate his brother. Nothing worked.

Reece had no will to live any longer. He had made the ultimate decision to stay in *The Keeping Place*. Now, he would never be able to return to the real world.

# CHAPTER THIRTY-SEVEN

James sat in the Care Center coffee shop, trying to put his thoughts together. He was trying to deal with his grief, when Kim came in and spotted him sitting alone at a table across the room. She walked across the room and asked him if she could join him.

"Yes, by all means, please do," he said, standing while she pulled out a chair and sat beside him. She had no idea that he had just lost his brother, or she would never have bothered him. She thought he was just taking a break from his busy schedule. She felt exhilarated because of Laurel's recovery, and she had left her side feeling assured that the nurses would watch over her while she slept. They would surely notify her if there were any changes. She was actually pleased to be able to talk to someone. James felt compelled to tell her about Reece.

He started, "That emergency, the reason I left you so abruptly, was a call to my brother's room. He..." He couldn't finish. He dropped his head in his hands and wept silently. Kim moved closer to him and put her arm around his shoulders. She assumed the worst, which was correct. He moved away slightly, and apologized for being unprofessional.

"He's your brother. Not just another patient. How could you feel anything less?"

"Well, I should be able to control my emotions better than this in public. I must pull myself together. I'll need to tell our mother. It will be very hard on her. I have to be strong for her."

"Would you like me to go with you? Would it help to have someone there with you?" she asked.

"Thank-you," he said sincerely. "That's the nicest thing anyone has ever offered to do for me, but no, I think this is something I must do by myself. Right now, we should probably go back up and look in on Laurel."

A tall lanky male nurse named Greg, sat by Laurel's bed watching her every move. He walked over by the door as another nurse, Rosalie came by. Rosalie was new at the Care Center, and Greg, being single had noticed right away. She looked cute with her white nurse's uniform on, and a little cleavage showed where the top button had been left undone. He had been trying to think up a way to talk to her, and the incident that had just happened was an opening. He motioned for her to come over to where he was standing. They began talking about the patient in the room down the hall. Laurel was listening. She had awakened, but had kept her eyes closed.

She heard some mumbling and then, "Did you know it was Dr. Martin's brother?" Greg asked Rosalie. Laurel listened more intently. She heard the name Martin, recognizing that it was Reece's last name also. *Was this a coincidence?* She thought. Her memories of the other world were still very clear, and they would remain this way for a short period of time and then, the memory of *The Keeping Place* would seem like a distant dream, and disappear completely within a few hours.

The nurses kept talking.

"He was a doctor too. I heard he got messed up on drugs. That's why he was in here. He overdosed on cocaine," Greg said. His approach was a little unusual, but it was opening a dialog between the two of them.

"Such a shame," Rosalie said. "He was a handsome man, from what I could see, and I understand he was really a good doctor before all of this happened. I saw him this morning right after I got here. We went on rounds on this floor first." Greg was feeling a little jealous of her response to another man, whether he was a patient or not. Even a dead one. He had obvious problems of insecurity that had never been resolved since childhood.

Rosalie was acting a little distant, but Greg was interested enough in her to answer her anyway, "Yes, Dr. Martin always expects the new help to take a special interest in this ward."

Rosalie said, "I've just come up to pick up his chart. They've already moved him down and taken him across to the morgue in the hospital."

195

Greg seemed shocked as he asked, "They didn't take his chart when they came to get him?"

"No, they tagged him, but somehow the chart got left behind," she said, as she walked down the hall two doors away and picked up the chart, leaving a card that stated who had been in the room previously. She walked back and stood by Greg for a moment, reading the chart.

Greg added, "He's been in here quite awhile. I'm surprised he has lasted this long. It's been almost three years. This is unusual, especially considering his condition when he came in. I've had to attend him on my shift quite often. You know there's always a lot of lifting and turning of these coma patients."

Rosalie nodded as she said, "Look, there's a piece of paper attached here, like a police report."

They both looked over the paper, as Greg said, "It says he assaulted a man…injured him pretty badly, but he lived. I don't think this paper is supposed to be in this chart. We'll have to ask Dr. Martin about this."

Rosalie said in a reflective mood, "Reece Martin, what a lovely name. Too bad he was really messed up," she sighed and walked on down the hall to deliver the chart. Greg smiled, and watched her slow and deliberate departure, unaware of the information he and Rosalie had just passed on to the patient lying in the room.

Laurel had heard all of this, and was devastated. They were clearly talking about her Reece. Tears welled up in her eyes, and she sobbed silently. She opened her eyes and tried to get up. She couldn't move. Her muscles had weakened lying in a bed for so many months, even with regular exercise from the staff. Somehow, it isn't quite the same as being able to sit up and walk. She could hear some commotion in the hallway. It was Kim and James returning to check on her. As they approached the bed, she tried to talk. The words were slow and deliberate, but very clear.

Almost in a whisper, she said, "I can't stay, I have to go back…to be with Reece." After hearing what the nurses had said, Laurel knew she had to go back to Reece. There was no way he would ever be able to come back now. He was gone forever from this world. Both James and Kim looked at each other in total amazement. They were confused at what she was saying, but they continued to listen intently.

Laurel knew that if she stayed any longer, she would begin to lose her memory of the other world, and would not remember why, or how to get back. If this was really what she wanted to do, she would have to make her move now. With this thought in her mind, the decision had been made, and then another force began pulling her, something strong, it was a good feeling. Her heart was making her decision now. With her last coherent breath she whispered, "Reece is...okay...I'll be with him...Don't worry...I'll be okay." Her eyes rolled back as a wisp of air escaped from her lips. Her eye lids twitched, and her body started to heave slightly as she slipped back into a comatose state.

James couldn't believe what he was seeing. In all his experience working with coma patients he had never seen anything like this. Although, he had seen people go back into comas, he had never seen anyone actually will themselves back into that condition, which was what he thought he had just witnessed. He quickly began examining her. He called the nurses for help. He gave her a shot of adrenalin, but it was too late, she was already gone. She was barely breathing, and had lapsed into a coma that appeared to be even deeper than the original one.

Laurel had done what she had set out to do. She knew she had to come back to her own world, if only for a moment in time. After hearing about Reece she knew she would never be happy without him. She had held onto the hope that somehow he would be able to come back too, but now, since he never could, she would have to return to him. She desperately hoped she had made the right decision, and just as she slipped back through *The Veil* she glanced at the clock on the wall it was exactly 11:11. She knew she had to go, now, and she did.

James examined Laurel thoroughly, and could find no reason for her to have gone back into a coma. He had seen other patients regress, but it was usually a slower process taking several days or weeks, and you could see a deterioration start to set in. They would appear to recover, and then regress slowly until one day, they just wouldn't wake up. In this case, there was nothing tangible to blame. She seemed the picture of health. James was wracked with grief from the death of his brother, and disillusioned by losing this patient from a relapse into a coma that held no reason. He had terrible feelings of inadequacy and hopelessness. He and Kim stayed by Laurel's side for awhile hoping she would open her eyes again and wake up, but she did not. They were both very confused by what she had said just before she relapsed. James couldn't understand why she would have mentioned Reece's name. He was sure there had never been any contact with the two of them. It was something that he and Kim would wonder about for a long time.

James had entertained thoughts before that maybe there was something going on inside the withering bodies of comatose patients, but he had no reality to base these theories on. It gave him hope to think that Reece might be somewhere in a better place. A place where he could be loved, happy, and whole again. It was just a thought.

Wearied from the episode that had just taken place, Kim had feelings of hopelessness too, but for other reasons. She could see no future at all for her friend. Feeling completely drained she started to leave the room, but as she walked close to James she looked up into his eyes. He reached out to her, and she fell into his arms. They held each other for a long time. These events had drawn them together for reasons neither of them knew. They needed each other more than ever now, for Kim had secretly made up her mind that it was over for Laurel. It was time to let go.

Laurel lived a few more hours in a deep coma, and then her will to live here in this world stopped, and her life ended. *Wherever Laurel was going,* Kim thought, *It must be a better place, her destiny has been fulfilled.* Kim searched her soul and finally felt relieved, without the guilt she had struggled with since the accident, because she knew this was something Laurel had apparently wanted to do. Laurel would live on in Kim's heart forever, and she felt privileged for having known her for the short time they had been friends. Kim thought, *A true friendship like we had is a treasure that I will always remember.* She and James left the hospital together feeling a sadness that needed no explanation. They had been drawn together under strange and unusual circumstances, and now they would find happiness that neither of them had really expected, but would both cherish.

Laurel and Reece left this existence, not because they had no choice, but because they did, indeed, have choices. Choices that, ultimately, would be for their well being. The very reason for existence in any world.

# CHAPTER THIRTY-EIGHT

Laurel, once again, found herself walking down a deserted highway. This time she wasn't afraid. She did feel some apprehension, wondering if she had done the right thing, but it was too late to change her mind now. She wondered, *Would Reece be waiting for her? Would she be able to find the love she yearned for? Would she be able to find happiness here in this place where she had felt confused and lost?* All these questions....unanswered.

She continued walking until she could see the little cafe down the road. *It isn't Nora's anymore,* she thought. Another person had replaced Nora. Maybe, Nora had gone back to the other world. She almost said, "My world" then realized that it wasn't her world anymore. This would be her world now. As she approached the cafe, she stood back, looked up and turned around several times before she reached for the door handle, when it opened, as if by itself. "Come right on in, honey," Nora said. "We've been expecting you."

Laurel gasped! "Nora? I thought you were gone."

"Well, I was gone for awhile, but I'm here now, and I'm really glad to see you. I have something to tell you that I think will make you very happy. There has always been this strong bond between us, and I was sent away to find out what that connection is, and I found it." Laurel had a puzzled look on her face as they hugged each other tightly, and Nora said, "I'll tell you later. Right now, there's someone waiting for you at that table over there." When Laurel looked across the room and saw Reece sitting there waiting just as he said he would be, she knew she had made the right choice. Her life wouldn't be the same, maybe not even what she had expected it to be, but she was with the love of her life. Together they would explore every wonderful thing, and live this life to the fullest, whatever it would bring. It was hard to imagine that she could have found happiness in this place where she least expected it. Not now, or ever again would she feel alienated and alone with Reece by her side. What once seemed like a nightmare had turned into a paradise. Love changes us in unusual ways. "Rosy Exposure" was happening again in *The Keeping Place*. And maybe, just maybe, in any world, that's a good thing.